Toolbelts & Ties

Working for Love, Book 2

Amber W. Lynne

Carnelian & Quills Publishing

Edited by: Krissy Espindola (KrissyEspindola@gmail.com)
Cover Art by: Rebecca Ruger (BeckandDot@gmail.com)
Paper: ISBN 978-1-960479-21-1
eBook: ISBN 978-1-960479-20-4
Text Copyright © 2025 by Carnelian & Quills Publishing
All rights reserved.

This book was for me...

It sparked an irresistible need to remind people that love is worth
working for and sometimes the most important person to love
is yourself <3

Chapter One

Molly

"You've got to be kidding me!"

Molly Monroe slammed her hand down on her desk hard enough to make the pens scattered across its polished surface bounce.

"No, I will not wait for him to call me," she snapped into the phone.

She stood, dragging her hand down her face as her Louboutin heels punctuated each word with a sharp click against the hardwood floor. "He was supposed to be there this morning. Today. Now."

Her fingers tightened around the phone as she turned toward the floor-to-ceiling windows that wrapped around her corner office. Her scowl stared back at her in the glass. Beyond it, a panoramic view of the Pacific Ocean stretched toward the Seattle skyline—Elliott Bay glittering beneath a thin veil of fog. NorthStar Properties had chosen this location carefully. Every inch of the space was designed to impress.

At the moment, it wasn't doing a damn thing to calm her nerves.

Molly took a deep breath and reached for the sugar. She hoped the woman on the other end of the line wasn't diabetic.

"Oh, right—thank you *so* much for your time. I'm incredibly grateful for your help," she said, her voice syrupy sweet. "Please let Mr. Beaumont know I truly need to speak with him. It's urgent. I need to talk to him as soon as he's available."

The moment she hung up, Molly let out a long, frustrated groan.

Her nails dug into her temples as she pressed against the headache forming there. Her therapist had been encouraging her to manage her stress levels.

"This is not helping," she muttered.

As if summoned by the thought, the message light on her phone blinked insistently. She pressed play without sitting back down.

"Hey, Molly, it's Paul. I heard work on the Calypso is delayed. We're starting soon, right?" His voice tightened. "This was already a tight timeline for the Christmas launch, and you know how important this project is. The junior partner spot is hinging on this happening. Call me back."

Molly closed her eyes and inhaled slowly—once, twice.

The chair squeaked as she pulled it out and dropped into it, pinching the bridge of her nose. Another delay would be disastrous. If Paul started questioning her leadership, the promotion she'd spent nearly eight years working toward would vanish—just like every other advancement that had gone to a Maherson son or an Ivy-League buddy.

"Pull it together, Monroe."

She uncapped the industrial-sized bottle of antacids hidden in her desk drawer, popped one into her mouth, and dialed Paul back.

The moment he answered, she was already reassuring him.

"Hi, Paul. No need to worry. Everything is moving along," she said smoothly. "I was just on the phone with Mr. Beaumont's office. They've assured me this project is a top priority."

She tapped her pen lightly against the desk. "The launch team confirmed we're still on schedule."

"I was under the impression things were stalled," Paul said carefully. "Should I be concerned?"

"Not at all," Molly replied, smiling despite the tight knot in her stomach. "This deal is solid. You can trust me."

The second the call ended, she slammed her phone onto the desk hard enough that it nearly bounced off.

A knock interrupted her silent scream.

She smoothed the wrinkles from her skirt and took a steadying breath. "Come in," she called. "Conner."

Her assistant poked his head through the doorway, his curly brown hair as wild as ever. "Uh-oh," he said, taking in her expression. "Do I need to clear your meetings for an emergency coffee run?"

"No. We don't have time for that." She exhaled. "I need you to handle a few things."

"Okay."

"I want you to follow up with Beaumont's office again. And call the suppliers."

Conner whistled softly. "Anything else?"

Molly glanced down at the calendar cluttered with meetings, fundraisers, networking lunches, and two half-hearted dinner dates with Mitchell. She circled the next week with her pen.

"I need you to cover for me."

"For the Calypso project?"

"Yes. The contractor hasn't started demolition yet. We're falling behind."

"Behind?" Conner blinked. "But you told Paul everything was fine."

"I lied." She clicked her pen twice and met his gaze. "Didn't your mother teach you not to eavesdrop?"

"I heard you yelling."

"Speaking forcefully."

"Why don't you just tell Mr. Maherson what's going on?"

Her jaw tightened. "I will not lose this promotion, Conner. I didn't work my way up for nearly eight years to watch it handed to someone who didn't earn it."

"I think he'd understand—"

"Make sure Paul doesn't find out we're behind schedule." Her hand went to her throat, the pressure there tightening until her voice rasped. "Please. Leave."

Conner nodded quickly and slipped out.

Molly dropped forward, her forehead hitting the desk.

A massage. A vacation. A miracle.

After three deep breaths, she opened her laptop. A new email notification blinked in the corner of the screen.

SUBJECT: You Forgot Me, Didn't You?

Molly shot upright so fast her knee slammed into the desk.

"Oh, hell."

Even though it was only three miles from her work, it still took twenty-five minutes to arrive at her favorite restaurant. Mama Malone's had been a lucky find the first year she'd arrived in Seattle. The small hole-in-the-wall Italian place had the best manicotti in town. The sauce was always thick with chunks of tomato and garlic, and, for an authentic Italian joint, they were surprisingly light on the oregano.

She circled twice before she could find a parking spot. "Please, please, please," she said, watching the clock on the dash. By the time she pulled into a parking spot, hopped out of the car, and trekked to the restaurant's entrance, she was a solid forty-five minutes late.

Mahogany wood and old red bricks merged with modern whitewashed walls. Red and white checkered plaid cloths covered the tables and wax dripped Chianti bottles lit up the room with flickering lights.

"Hey, Molly." The host greeted her. "You're late."

"Wow, thanks for the announcement, Fillipe."

He lifted a single dark eyebrow. "Really late."

"Save it." With a quick scan of the room, she lifted a brow. "Usual spot?"

"Yeah."

"Thanks." Walking into the back of the restaurant, she passed a young couple, both with beaming smiles on their faces.

A family with three young children sat at a nearby table.

Pasta sauce covered the youngest from head to toe. In the dark shadows, near the back, sat a small round table. Mitchell was sitting there watching her.

"Mitch," she said, as she dropped into the seat across from him. "I'm so sorry."

His tailored shirt pulled tight against his biceps when he leaned forward, grabbed her seat, and pulled it out for her. "Sit."

Words started tumbling from her mouth even before her butt hit the chair. "Honestly, if you only knew. I'm drowning with the Calypso project."

Her words filled the space between them like packing fluff: all the reasons she was late, a few more apologies, and a plea for him to understand tumbled out of her mouth. When she'd stopped talking, he continued to sit silently. Laughter and whispered voices floated between them, softening the silence, but she needed him to speak. "Mitchell?"

He leaned back, arms loosely crossed. His voice was calm. Too calm. "On our *anniversary*, Molly?"

Her stomach twisted. "I got caught up!" Looking at the morsels of food left on the plates in front of her, she asked, "Did you eat without me?"

"I did."

"Oh, okay. I'm glad that you didn't go hungry. It wasn't intentional. Honest."

"I understand. It never is."

Nodding her head like a bobble doll, she said, "We can celebrate our anniversary this weekend." She reached out to take his hand. "You know I love you."

"I love you, too." He leaned forward, forearms braced on

the table. "Molly, I've been thinking about this for months."

She swallowed. "Thinking about *what*?"

Mitchell slid his hand into his pocket, and her breath caught. He pulled out something small...box-shaped.

She sucked in a breath. *Oh God. Was this it? Was he finally...*

Then he set it down.

Not a ring.

A key.

Her apartment key.

Her heart stopped.

"I'm done," he said simply.

Her mouth parted, but no words came out.

"Here's your key back. I don't want to do this anymore."

"Wh...What?"

"You heard me. I'm done."

"Just like that?"

"There is no 'just like that,' Molly." He pushed back in his seat so hard the legs squeaked on the floor. "How many times have you forgotten me? How many countless meals have I eaten alone? Our relationship isn't a business transaction." He didn't sound angry, just exhausted. "You keep putting me second. Or third. Or fourth behind your endless *meetings*. And I kept making excuses for you."

"I do! God knows I do, but it'll be a little longer and then I'll make partner. Then this will be something we laugh about. You know, it's just the hard times."

"I don't think it is. With the promotion, you'll be even busier and gone even more. What would you do if we had kids? Hell, did you even notice I got a dog?"

"What? What does a dog have to do with any of this?" She glanced around at the surrounding tables. Tens of faces were staring back at her. Their hands were holding forks and spoons full of food that were sitting in mid-air and the drama fascinated them. Molly looked back at Mitchell. "Please don't do this..."

"It's done. Thanks for dinner," he said, placed his napkin on the table as he stood up. Carefully, he pushed in his chair. "You can keep this place. I know it's your favorite, but Mae's Cafe is mine." He began to walk away and then paused. She reached for him, but he brushed off her arm. "Call me in a week or two. I'll have your stuff packed and waiting for you." Without another word, he walked away, leaving her sitting there with her jaw hanging down and her mouth gaping open.

As the sounds of the restaurant returned to normal, she remained quiet in her seat. The surrounding customers had returned to their meals. Then they would return to their homes. What would she return to?

Fillipe asked, "You still want to eat? I could get you something to go."

She jumped a bit in her chair, startled by the words spoken over her shoulder. "The manicotti, a caesar salad, and two orders of the tiramisu. I'll eat it here."

"You sure?" he said, glancing around at the other patrons in the restaurant.

"Yes, I'm not ready to head home, not yet."

Placing his hand on her shoulder, he squeezed gently. "We've got you covered. I'll let Pa know to make it extra tasty tonight."

"Thanks Fillipe, you may be the only decent man left in my

life."

He shot her a crooked smile. "Shame I'm already taken."

"Frankie's a lucky guy." Though her throat was slowly pinching tighter, she kept the pooling tears at bay. "Can you go get me my dessert?" Candlelight caught the sharp curve of her chin as she tilted her face towards him and asked, "I'll take the manicotti home."

For a moment, he paused next to her, then he shook his head, and said, "Of course," before he walked through the swinging doors that led to the kitchen.

Chapter Two

Molly

"Stupid," Molly said, and buried her face in her pillows, but the five-hundred-thread-count Egyptian cotton sheets felt like sandpaper against her swollen eyelids.

She'd wallowed last night. *Hard.*

A bottle of wine. A dozen replays of Celine Dion's *All By Myself,* and the overwhelming silence of an empty bed.

His words clawed against the inside of her skull, "*You don't listen.*"

It had been calm...*rehearsed.*

Except she *had* been listening. She'd always been listening, maybe not *well,* because she was also *planning for their future.*

She knew she should have seen it coming. The signs had all been there: missed goodnight texts that once came like clock-work, visits that grew shorter, peppered with weak excuses, and canceled date nights that had stacked up like unpaid bills. With each excuse, she convinced herself things weren't so terrible. *Work's been crazy,* she reasoned. *He'll understand.*

The smell of his cologne still lingered in the air, a cruel ghost of his morning routine. He used to shower, steam curling into the hallway, as he casually recounted his plans for the day.

She looked up at the ceiling, fighting back tears. She fixated on his words, wondering what she'd missed and what she could have done to change things. But deep down, she knew the truth: it wasn't *all* her fault. She had been stupid to think he'd understand her need to balance work and life, but she'd also believed in love...that they could work it all out. Was that so wrong?

She glared at the sun beaming in through the bedroom window. Usually, Mitch would have closed it before they went to sleep.

When the alarm started blaring by her head, she said, "Molly, stop being ridiculous. Get up."

She inhaled sharply, swinging her legs out of the bed before she could let herself spiral any further. "You do not have time for this."

In the bathroom, his toothbrush, shaving cream, and hair pomade rested on the counter next to the sink. With a broad sweep, she pulled it all together and slid it into the trash. "Like you did to us."

With robotic efficiency, she moved through the motions of her morning. Anytime her mind wandered, she'd shake her head. "Stop it."

In a daze, she moved from the bathroom to the kitchen. There, too, lay the remnants of her shattered relationship. A framed photo sat on the counter next to the coffeemaker. But then—Her fingers faltered on the countertop when she glanced down at the framed picture resting next to the coffeemaker.

Mitchell held Molly in his arms. His wavy brown hair had been blowing in the beach breeze and she'd let her hair down that day. Tendrils of her curly blonde hair were blowing back into his face. Their blue and brown eyes flashed in the summer sun and small wrinkles pinched the corners where they squinted. *Carefree.*

Her stomach twisted sharply, and before she could second-guess it, she flipped the frame face-down on the counter.

She sent up a prayer for whoever had invented automatic coffee makers and poured a cup. Grabbing her phone off the charger, she turned it on.

As she took a fortifying sip of coffee, she turned on her phone. A chorus of pings and missed call alerts exploded across her screen. Her stomach dropped.

Call Me Now.

Urgent.

She barely had time to scan the urgent messages before her phone rang. Molly winced when she saw the name. *Mr. Maherson.*

"Finally." His voice was abrupt when she answered.

"Good morning, Mr. Maherson," she said, already rubbing her temples.

"It's morning, but I wouldn't call it good."

"Oh, no—"

"Wait. I need an update. I called Paul, He told me *you* were the lead on the Calypso Hotel expansion. Is there a reason I had to hear that from him?"

Molly bit back an exasperated groan. *Paul.* Of course, he would throw her name out first instead of handling it himself.

"Yes, sir," she said. "I've been managing the project—"

"Then perhaps you can explain why Mr. Beaumont called me this morning apologizing that your project *still* hasn't broken ground?"

"He called you?" she asked, struggling to keep her voice steady.

Maherson scoffed. "No, *he* called *you*. But when he couldn't reach you, your assistant patched him through to me."

Her pulse throbbed in her skull. *Conner.* That...traitorous, day-ruining little...

"I spoke to his office yesterday!" she argued quickly. "Ana, his secretary, told me this was his top priority. I assumed that meant—"

"You assumed?" Maherson's voice went ice cold.

Molly shut her eyes, backtracking immediately. "No, sir. I misunderstood. I *will* handle this."

"Not good enough, Ms. Monroe."

She blinked. "Sir?"

"You're going to Texas. I want in you Serenity...today."

Her stomach flipped. "I—*what*?"

"I don't think I was unclear. If you can't get this moving from your office, you'll need to do it in person. I expect you to get moving, now."

"Sir, I...we...there's no need for me to travel."

"There is now." His voice left no room for discussion. "And I expect a full status update when you arrive in Houston tonight. Understood?"

Molly swallowed hard, her knuckles white around her coffee mug. "Understood, Mr. Maherson."

The line clicked.

When the click sounded on the line, it took every calming technique her therapist had taught her to resist throwing the stupid, expensive iPhone across the room. Instead, she took three deep breaths, counted to ten, and said, "I am enough. I can do this," and dialed her office.

The traitor picked up on the first ring. "Hello, Ms. Monroe's office. How can—"

"Conner. Why the hell did you put Maherson through to Beaumont?"

There was a hesitation. "I couldn't reach you."

"Did you try my home line?"

"No?"

"I live five minutes from the office. Knock on my door!"

"That's not, uh, technically in my job descri—"

"It is *literally* your job."

A sheepish pause. "Well, in my defense, Mr. Beaumont really needed to talk to someone."

Molly resisted the urge to bang her forehead against the wall.

Instead, she ground out, "Cancel my entire schedule for the week. Book me a first-class ticket to Houston, a hotel, and transportation—for *today*. I don't care about the cost, book it."

"Y-Yes, ma'am!" Conner squeaked.

Molly exhaled sharply. *Good.*

She hung up the call. She wanted to toss the phone against the wall. Instead, she threw it down on her bed as she walked into her closet.

If the day had started horribly, the flight itself was actual, certified hell.

The older gentleman in front of her reclined his chair so far back she could study the *exact* point where his toupee didn't quite blend with his real hair.

A baby cried for three straight hours, and, to top it all off, Conner had booked her flying in coach.

Dragging her suitcase through the Houston terminal, she bumped into an airport chair and stubbed her toe so hard she saw stars. She fumbled for her phone, pulling up Conner's itinerary email.

Rental: RESERVED — Pick up at the airport.

Of course. He was going to need an entire retraining in travel planning when she got home.

She limped toward the rental counters, jaw clenched, and repeated under her breath, "You do not have time for this."

By the time she'd found the rental counter, signed the paperwork, and wrestled her luggage into the trunk, she was exhausted, frustrated, and in desperate need of a drink.

She pulled out her phone, preparing to rally for another round of calls, when she glimpsed the sun setting outside.

"Oh, no. Time zones."

Her phone lit up. It was 7 p.m., and she hadn't made her promised call to Mr. Maherson.

Panic jolted through her, and she checked the GPS. "How far to the hotel?" she muttered.

Almost an hour.

"An hour?" Cursing, she whipped out her phone and called Maherson.

He answered on the second ring.

"You're late, Monroe."

Molly clenched her jaw. "Yes, sir. I've just arrived in Houston. I'm on my way to a local hotel and I'll meet with Mr. Beaumont first thing in the morning."

A long pause. "Fine. Keep me updated."

The line went dead.

Molly finally exhaled, leaned back against the seat, and let the exhaustion steamroll her.

If she had to fight every stubborn contractor in Texas to prove she could...so be it.

Chapter Three

Molly

The heat hit her the second she stepped off the plane.

Not warmth. Not sunshine. Heat.

It wrapped around Molly like a damp blanket, heavy and unrelenting, clinging to her silk blouse before she'd even reached the terminal doors. She paused, blinking against the brightness, her sunglasses fogging instantly as Texas made its presence known.

So much for a quick refresh before the meeting.

She tugged at the collar of her blouse and adjusted her blazer, already regretting every fashion choice she'd made that morning. Seattle had been crisp. Controlled. Predictable.

Serenity was none of those things.

By the time she reached the rental car, her heels clicked irritably against the concrete, the sharp sound echoing in the open-air garage. Her Louboutins—chosen for confidence, authority, and a subtle reminder of who she was—felt suddenly impractical.

Ridiculous, even.

Molly slid into the driver's seat and cranked the air conditioning to its highest setting, gripping the steering wheel as she pulled up the GPS. The directions loaded slowly, the signal stuttering.

Of course it did.

The highway gave way to narrower roads, the city thinning until it disappeared entirely. Strip malls turned into feed stores. Office parks into open fields. She rolled her window down halfway, immediately regretted it, and rolled it back up again.

Dust swirled behind pickup trucks. Mud splattered the sides of her rental car as she followed a detour sign that looked as though it had been nailed into the ground sometime around the Carter administration.

"This cannot be correct," she muttered.

Her phone buzzed in the cup holder. No signal.

Perfect.

She checked her reflection in the rearview mirror. Her makeup was still flawless, but the effort suddenly felt misplaced—like wearing a cocktail dress to a backyard barbecue. Sweat beaded at her temples, threatening her carefully controlled appearance.

This was supposed to be a straightforward site visit.

Instead, the road ahead narrowed further, the pavement uneven, potholes filled with murky water from a recent storm. Molly slowed instinctively, watching brown splashes fan out dangerously close to her shoes as the car lurched forward.

Mud. Actual mud.

She exhaled sharply through her nose. "You are a professional. You can handle this."

A sign appeared ahead:

WELCOME TO SERENITY

Hand-painted. Slightly crooked.

Molly stared at it as she passed, her grip tightening on the wheel.

She had walked into boardrooms filled with men twice her age who'd underestimated her. She'd negotiated multi-million-dollar contracts without breaking a sweat. She'd survived corporate politics, late nights, and a promotion path designed to test endurance rather than merit.

And yet, as she drove deeper into town—past quiet storefronts, parked trucks, and people who waved at one another for no apparent reason—she couldn't shake the feeling that she'd stepped into a world operating on an entirely different clock.

Slower.

Deliberate.

Unimpressed by resumes or designer shoes.

Molly straightened in her seat.

Fine. She could adapt.

She always did.

Reaching the jobsite, Molly flung open the car door and leaped out as the car jolted into park. The moment her heels hit the gravel lot, she stopped short. "Oh. No."

Tall enough to block the sun, the six-story building towered over her. The siding was warped and cracked. Its paint had long since faded to an unappealing shade of beige, blending too well with the thick humidity and smog hanging in the air. The building had seen more than one hurricane and had not fared well.

The windows were dark, hazy, or broken. There were countless piles of debris next to a sad excuse for a fountain filled with murky, stagnant water. "No." Her stomach twisted. "If the outside looks this bad, what does the inside look like?"

All the project reports she'd seen had shown the hotel needed 'extensive updates.' This wasn't an update. This was a demolition project disguised as a renovation.

Why hadn't she been told?

Her fingers clenched at her sides. Paul had either severely downplayed the damage, or their project procurement team needed to reevaluate their job qualification.

Either way, she should have been here weeks ago.

Anger surged through her, but she shoved it down for now. *Focus.*

Molly could hear the sounds of men talking in the distance. Following their voices, she found a group of men wearing orange hats and yellow vests standing together near the edge of what was, sadly, being called a pool. Calling it a putrid waste heap would have been more fitting.

"Hello?" As they all turned to face her, she picked out Mr. Beaumont from the group. She didn't even have to ask if it was him. The way he held his shoulders told her he thought he was the boss. He had all the familiar traits of a powerful man. The sharpness of his jaw, the confident stance, the practiced indifference as he caught sight of her storming toward him.

Molly squared her shoulders.

"Mr. Beaumont!"

He responded to his name, brows lifting slightly. Small tufts of blond hair peeked out from underneath his hard hat and shadowy gray eyes met hers. Then—to her absolute irritation—he smirked.

"You must be Ms. Monroe." The way his eyes scrutinized her clashed with the casual Texan drawl in his deep voice.

Molly extended her hand, professional but firm. *Control the conversation.* "I need to speak with you about the Calypso Hotel project."

Jackson shook her hand, a surprisingly solid grip. Then, without hesitation, he pulled a bright yellow hard hat from a nearby crate and dropped it onto her head.

Molly sputtered, pushing the crooked helmet up off her forehead. "Excuse me?"

"Restricted area." His mouth tugged slightly upward, just enough to mock her flustered confusion.

Molly counted to three. *Do not strangle him.*

"I...appreciate the concern," she bit out. "But Mr. Beaumont, I came all the way from Seattle to ensure this project stays on schedule."

"Ahhh, it'll be fine," he said, and waved his hand. "Y'all can't help getting worked up about everything."

As he began walking towards the gate, she ran after him, stumbling a bit in the rocks while rotting leaves and mud grabbed at her feet. "You can't give me an hour of your time?"

Jackson turned, already walking toward the gates. "I've already been here for three hours."

Molly's pulse spiked. He was leaving? "Could you spare a half hour, then?"

"I could. But I won't."

Oh, this man is absolutely impossible.

"Mr. Beaumont—"

"Ma'am," he said, cutting her off. "I run several projects. This one ain't my only priority."

Her nostrils flared. "This is a—"

"Best way to keep your project on track is to show up before things fall apart," Jackson said, unfazed. "Maybe set that alarm a little earlier next time."

Molly, driven by determination and a relentless work ethic, was speechless.

"Construction starts early. My crew works best before the sun is beating down on them, and we can't wait for you. Try sacrificing some of that beauty sleep and make it here a little earlier tomorrow." Beaumont's gaze flickered down and his firm jaw twitched. He looked down, appraising her, his smile barely contained. Being about ten inches taller made it an effortless task. "Not that it ain't working for you."

This was, hands down, the single most infuriating interaction of her career.

She stood in the middle of a year's worth of garbage and trash, watching him walk away.

A tap on her shoulder caught her attention, and she turned to see an older gentleman standing behind her. "The boss is always a little short at the beginning of a project. He likes to know that everything is working out all right."

"Then he should have started days ago like he promised!"

"Maybe," said the contractor, tipping the edge of his hard hat towards her. "I can give you a tour if you'd like."

"I would like that," Molly said, trying to look humble. "Thank you."

The man reached out his hand, his rough fingers scraped against her soft skin. "Name's Duncan. It's a pleasure to meet you."

She shook his hand, marveled at how polite they were in the South, and said, "The pleasure's mine." The trash, his boss's tantrum, or her questionable attire would not derail Duncan's good manners.

He took her towards the hotel as two large trucks backed up to drop dumpsters into the parking lot while crews of men began gathering in corners with fifty-gallon black contractor bags. "They'll have this taken care of in no time. Any real Houstonian knows how to clean up after a storm. We come together here."

"I hope so..." she said, watching the crews until Duncan showed her through the front doors. "No..." her throat caught on the stench in the air. There were rotting carpets and dead plants, moldy paper and decaying linens. The earthy smell of mildew permeated the air. Stepping back, she said, "Should we be breathing this?"

"Here." Duncan was ready. He handed her a mask to pull over her face. Glad there was no one to take a picture of her done up in her safety gear and high-end business fashion, she swore she would wear something more practical the next day.

Further inside, she stumbled, a cracked, peeling linoleum tile catching her foot. "Stupid heels."

"Should I get a guy to loan you a pair of boots?"

"Duncan, thank you. Truly, but I can't do this today. I want to contact the office in Seattle, get some fresh ideas and come back to this tomorrow."

"Might not be a bad idea, miss. Then you could wear some real clothes while you're at it."

"If I'd had some warning—"

A shout from outside caught Duncan's attention. He held up his hand and guided her back towards the door. "I need to check on this, and I don't want to leave you alone in here."

He led her through the lobby's rubble, to the pool area on the entrance's left. With thoughtful landscaping, it would be an alluring feature for guests entering the building for events and check-in. Without greenery, it was nothing more than a skate park next to a dirty, old parking lot.

Jackson, and another worker, peered into the pool. A third guy was in the pit's bottom with a massive shovel. "Hey, we found a dead armadillo in here!"

"Can't you two grow up? You know what to do." Jackson waved at the rotting pile in the pool's bottom. "Take it out, give it a decent burial, and then get back to work." Jackson turned towards her. "Still here, huh?"

"Yes, there's a lot to be done. Duncan showed me inside—"

"I'm sorry. Can I take you around more tomorrow?" He said, before interrupting her. "It'll be calmer then and you can..." he looked her up and down, "find something more fitting to wear."

"You may be on to something there." Molly waved to the old contractor as he directed the guy in the hole. "Thanks for your help today, Duncan."

"Any time," he grunted and waved back, before pointing at a dirty pile of leaves and yelling, "Get that, too! I think it's moving."

She looked back at Jackson and asked, "When should I show up?"

"Six tomorrow."

Jackson hummed in acknowledgment. "Oh, and bring coffee."

Molly let her frustration pour out then, squaring her shoulders. She checked her watch.

Less than twenty-four hours before, she had to prove exactly why she was the one in charge.

God help Jackson Beaumont when she did.

Chapter Four

Molly

Molly hadn't meant to spend the afternoon shopping. But, after surviving the disastrous walk around the Calypso Hotel job site in her impractical heels, she'd pulled out her phone and searched for somewhere selling—*anything*—that could pass as functional footwear.

That's how she ended up between a quaint hardware store and a heavenly-smelling bakery at a small store called A Stitch in Time. The hand-painted wooden sign above the storefront gave it an intimate, unexpected charm.

Molly opened the front door and stepped inside. The shop was a kaleidoscope of textures and colors. Sunlight streamed through the large front window, catching on shimmering fabrics and the glint of delicate rings and necklaces displayed in glass cases. A faint floral scent—citrus and sandalwood—lingered in the air.

The realization that this was no ordinary small-town store hit her. Molly hadn't expected to find L.A. fashion in the middle of Serenity, Texas, but that's what she got when the shop's owner emerged from behind the counter.

"Welcome, honey," a rich, smooth voice said. "You lost, or are you about to make the best fashion decision of your life?"

Molly blinked as the woman—tall, chic, and unbothered—grinned at her.

"I'm Taylor, welcome to A Stitch in Time." With her flawless embroidery-covered crop top, high-waisted jeans, and a silver cuff glinting on her wrist, she looked like she had an effortless style embedded into her DNA. "What can I help you find?"

"I...uh, need jeans," Molly admitted, aware of her mud-streaked slacks and broken pride.

Taylor didn't even flinch. "Sweetheart, you've come to the right place."

For the next thirty minutes, Taylor subjected Molly to a personal styling intervention. She had an uncanny ability to pair personality, practicality, and enough sparkle to make Molly second-guess everything she thought she knew about denim.

"No." Molly scowled at a pair of jeans with rhinestones down the back pockets.

"Yes," Taylor corrected, tossing them onto the fitting room bench.

Taylor swept Molly into a whirlwind of denim for another thirty minutes. She had her trying on jeans with floral embroidery, pairs with subtle fringe, and even a high-waisted style Molly initially turned her nose up at—until she caught sight of herself in the full-length mirror.

"You're working it!" Taylor said, laughter ringing out as she handed over another pair.

By the time Molly emerged, she was grinning like a fool, feeling like she'd walked a runway in some Southern spin-off of *Vogue*. She came out four pairs of pants richer and slightly dazzled by her own reflection. And the boots? *Oh, the boots.* The perfect, buttery-soft leather, hand-stitched as if by angels, hugged her ankles.

When Taylor handed her the bags, she winked. "You'll thank me later."

Molly wasn't so sure about that, but as she left, she couldn't quite bring herself to regret her spending spree, either.

Back at the hotel, Molly sank into a stiff armchair and braced herself for her next battle. The moment she dialed Paul's number, he picked up. "Molly, finally. What's happening down there?"

"You mean besides the fact that I walked into a project that should have been labeled 'structural disaster' instead of 'light renovation'?" She exhaled. "Why didn't we know how bad this was?"

He hesitated. "The location is excellent, and the historical architecture is appealing—"

"Sure, the location isn't bad, I'll give you that, but the hotel is a *wreck*. I'm thinking a full demolition would've been better than a remodel. And, now, there's no time for that." Molly squeezed her eyes shut for a moment. "Floorboards are rotting, ceilings are caving, and the pool?" She let out a humorless laugh. "It's basically an unfiltered swamp."

"Look, it's not ideal, but Jackson Beaumont lives for projects like this. He has a reputation."

"So do disaster movies. I wouldn't invest in one hoping for a happy ending," said Molly, as she shook her head.

"Fair." Paul said, "But seriously, Mr. Maherson trusts him. You just need to do your job and make sure this stays on track."

"That's what I'm worried about. Mr. Beaumont seems a tad overconfident. Thank God he lives in Texas because his ego is too big to fit anywhere else." Molly tapped her nails against the desk, filing that answer away. "Fine. I'll watch him."

"That's what you do best, Monroe," Paul said, before ending the call.

Molly tossed her phone onto the desk with a little too much force.

She was supposed to 'keep an eye' on Jackson, but that man wielded charm as a blunt weapon. She wasn't about to let him smooth-talk his way around deadlines.

Control. That's what she needed...and time.

"What would your therapist tell you?" She stared up at the ceiling of her hotel room. "Don't talk to yourself. She wouldn't say that. Like arguing with that hunk of man muscle isn't enough. Now, I'm arguing with myself. Molly Monroe, get your act together."

As she looked around the room, she realized the light had dimmed. "Time zones." Molly swore and pulled on her new sneakers. "Find some food and get ready for another day. You'll have another chance at beating Beaumont tomorrow."

Walking helped clear her mind and the late afternoon sun wrapped the small town's Main Street in golden light. A light breeze carried the smell of fresh pastries from somewhere near-by.

She walked slowly, taking in the town's details. Serenity wasn't full of steel and high rises. Instead, the buildings had old brick facades, flower boxes in the windows, and hand-painted signs.

Serenity moved at a pace Molly found both unsettling and impossible to ignore.

She noticed it immediately as she stepped onto Main Street, the heat already pressing down but without the frantic urgency she was used to back home. People didn't rush. They didn't glance at their phones every five seconds or weave through foot traffic with clipped apologies.

They stopped. They talked. They lingered.

Molly paused just outside the café, her reflection faint-ly visible in the glass. Inside, ceiling fans turned lazily, their steady rhythm cutting through the hum of quiet conversation. A chalkboard menu leaned against the wall instead of hanging straight. No one seemed bothered by it.

She checked her watch.

Still on schedule.

That, somehow, made it worse.

The bell above the café door chimed softly as she stepped inside. The smell of coffee—rich, unhurried, un-burnt—wrapped around her. A woman behind the counter smiled as if she had nowhere else to be and all the time in the world.

"Well, hey there," she said warmly. "What can I get you, honey?"

Molly blinked, momentarily thrown by the lack of rehearsed efficiency. "Coffee. Black. Please."

The woman nodded, unbothered. "Take a seat. I'll bring it right over."

Take a seat.

Molly hesitated, then chose a small table near the window. Outside, a man leaned against a lamppost, chatting with another who showed no sign of leaving. Across the street, someone unlocked a shop door at least ten minutes past the posted opening time—and no one complained.

This town operated on trust instead of urgency.

The realization settled uneasily in her chest.

She pulled out her phone, then stopped. No missed calls. No emails demanding updates. No calendar reminders screaming for attention.

For the first time in days, there was nothing immediately pulling at her.

Her coffee arrived moments later, set gently in front of her.

"Let me know if you need anything else," the woman said. "No rush."

Molly wrapped her hands around the mug. It was warm. Solid. Real.

Slow didn't mean lazy, she reminded herself.It meant intentional.

She took a sip and looked out the window again, watching Serenity move at its own unbothered pace.

Kids rode bikes down the sidewalk, laughing loud enough

to echo. A couple sat across from each other at an outdoor café, hands tangled between coffee cups. Nothing felt rushed. She wasn't used to this kind of space. She wasn't sure how she felt about it.

But...it wasn't *bad*.

By the time she sank into bed that night, her new boots sat by the door, ready waiting for whatever chaos tomorrow would bring.

Molly felt fed, full, and a little less alone. Serenity, Texas, felt unfamiliar, but the slow, deliberate way of living steadied her.

Tomorrow, she'd face Beaumont and his Texas-sized ego. But for tonight, she pulled the comforter up to her chin, thinking Taylor might have had a point.

She might end up turning heads after all.

Chapter Five

Jackson

When Jackson's truck tires crunched across the Calypso Hotel's parking lot, early morning light stretched long shadows across the construction site. A handful of trucks were already parked, but the space was still mostly quiet. He liked mornings like this—the calm before the day's noise set in. It gave him room to think. To plan.

Duncan was waiting near his own truck, clipboard in hand, posture relaxed like he had nowhere else to be. "Morning, Boss. Got here early to check on the guys. They've been working hard."

Jackson nodded, taking in the steady rhythm of the site waking up. "That's what I like to hear. Any issues overnight?"

Duncan shook his head. "Nope. Materials are on schedule. Crew's ready."

"Perfect." Jackson scanned the property, the familiar satisfaction of a job underway settling in his chest. "I need to—"

His phone rang, cutting him off. One glance at the screen

told him it wasn't a call he could ignore. "Excuse me, Duncan. I've got to take this."

He stepped away, boots crunching over gravel, and answered. "Beaumont here."

"Jackson, it's Ana." Her voice was tight. "There's a problem. The temporary repairs from last week didn't hold. Roof started leaking."

Jackson's jaw set. "Ana. I thought we had this handled."

"I know. I'm sorry. I'll start making calls, see if we can get someone out there sooner."

"You know the Calypso's kicking off. I needed—" He dragged a hand through his hair, then stopped himself. The work would get done; it always did. "No. It's not on you. Just try to get it sorted."

A beat. "Of course. But I know you, Jackson. You're not going to ignore this."

He glanced back at the hotel, its worn exterior softened by the morning light. "I'll fix it," he said, and ended the call.

Duncan was watching him, arms crossed, expression knowing. "Problems, Boss?"

Jackson shifted his weight, tone even. "Nothing worth worrying about. Minor delay. I'll handle it."

Duncan nodded. He didn't look convinced, but he didn't push. "Figured today your priority was Ms. Molly."

Jackson checked his watch. Yeah. Molly would be here soon. And she wouldn't like waiting. "She is," he said, sliding his phone into his pocket. "She's just going to have to wait a bit. This comes first."

"Alright." Duncan studied him, then shrugged. "Pretty

sure Ms. Molly likes me. I'll show her a little Southern charm. She won't even remember you were supposed to be here."

"There's a lot you're good at, old man," Jackson said, clapping him on the shoulder, "but I don't think you're her type."

Duncan hooted. "You think you are?"

"Work, Duncan. This is work," Jackson called back, though the words rang less solid than he meant them to.

"Don't worry. I've got Ms. Molly and the crew covered. You do what you need to do."

Jackson climbed into his truck. "You're a lifesaver. Tell her I'll update her as soon as I can. I'll try to swing back later."

Molly would be upset. Especially if she'd brought coffee. But Duncan had a way of smoothing rough edges. His charm worked on just about everyone.

Jackson took one last look at the Calypso before pulling out. The hotel wasn't just a job. It was tied to Serenity—to the people, the place, the life he'd built. He hadn't been avoiding Molly because he couldn't handle her, or because the project didn't matter.

He just needed time.

Today, he couldn't afford to let personal feelings bleed into responsibility. Still, as he turned onto the road, it felt like he was leaving something behind at the site—waiting for her arrival.

Chapter Six

Molly

She wasn't exactly expecting Jackson Beaumont to greet her with a project binder and a charming smile, but she had expected him to at least be there.

Instead, Duncan stood in the middle of the job site, looking perfectly at ease, tipping his hardhat in greeting. "Ms. Molly, you look ready to work today."

"Yeah, well," Molly lifted the heel of her new boots, "figured I'd have better luck in these than heels."

Duncan let out a low chuckle. "A wise decision."

She took a slow sip of her pumpkin spice latte—the closest thing she could get to real coffee this morning—and scanned the site. Even with the early morning humidity weighing down her hair, her nerves were sharp, and she was ready to get started.

"Where's Mr. Beaumont?" she asked, shifting onto her other foot.

Duncan scratched his beard, glancing toward the already-active crew. "Oh, he came by early. Checked in around six, gave us our orders, and left."

Molly nearly choked on her coffee. "What?"

"He showed up this morning, told me how to direct the men, and left. He's a busy man, Mr. Jack."

All the warm, fuzzy feelings her morning coffee had given her vanished.

Before she could respond, Duncan kept talking. "Don't you worry, though. He told me to finish up the tour with you and answer your questions."

"Is he avoiding me?"

"I don't think so..."

"Will I see him tomorrow?"

"I can't make a promise on that."

Molly exhaled slowly—counting to five to avoid strangling the first available construction worker. Maybe it was the sunrise cresting over the Calypso Hotel, maybe it was pure frustration; either way, she saw red.

She forced herself to breathe, then looked back at Duncan's patient face. "I'm sorry. I desperately need to speak with him."

"I understand, miss, but let's start with that tour."

Molly followed him through halls lined with years of neglect. Crumbled drywall, mold-speckled wallpaper, and the ghosts of better days lingered everywhere she looked.

"The bones are good," Duncan assured her as they climbed the stairs. "We'll reinforce everything before build-out starts."

She nudged aside a loose tile and moved deeper into the

building. Water stains bloomed across the ceiling, and she tugged her dust mask higher. Once-grand walls sagged and crumbled, the hotel reduced to exposed structure and debris.

The lobby was in the same state of disrepair she'd seen the day before. While crews had made visible progress outside—clearing debris and staging materials—the interior remained untouched.

"Once demo starts in earnest, things will move fast," Duncan said. "We're also installing updated security—cameras, controlled access points, the works. Keeps vandals out and protects the crew once equipment's on-site."

Molly nodded absently, filing the note away as she scanned the space.

They passed the ballrooms, where ragged curtains drooped and water lines crept up the walls.

"Careful on those stairs," Duncan said as he guided her upward. "Elevator should be running in about a week."

"That soon?"

"We've got generators powering select areas. Structural work comes first. This old girl's taken a beating."

"What are the worst areas?"

"You've seen them. Mr. Beaumont figures once we get the lobby stabilized, the rest will come together lickety-split."

Molly could see the vision beneath the decay—the elegance waiting to be uncovered. Still, the scale of the work made her stomach dip.

Lower floors bore the worst water damage. Higher up, the problems shifted to age and neglect—varmints, leaks, dust-coated rooms frozen in time.

As Duncan talked through Beaumont's plans, Molly understood why Jackson trusted him. His confidence was grounded, earned.

She imagined cabanas, fire pits, guests laughing beneath strings of lights. Not yet—but soon.

What still bothered her was Jackson's absence. He was treating this like a solo act, not a partnership. She wanted in. On everything.

Once the tour wrapped up, dusty but energized, Molly thanked Duncan and headed back to her rental car, already pulling her keys from her pocket.

It was time to confront her contractor.

Molly marched into Jackson's office, determination sharpening every step.

"Welcome to—"

"Is he in?"

"You must be Ms. Monroe. I'm Ana," said the woman behind the desk, standing to shake her hand. She had thick dark hair, warm brown skin, and an ease that felt wildly out of place in a construction office.

"Is Mr. Beaumont here?" Molly asked again.

Ana tapped her pen. "Nope."

"Then I'll wait."

She gestured toward the chairs. "Suit yourself. Might be a while."

Grinding her teeth, Molly folded her arms. "Fine."

Ana smirked, unfazed, and returned to her paperwork.

"While I'm waiting, I'd like to review the Calypso remodel plans."

"Oh, he keeps most of that in his head," Ana said. "We've got the architect's drafts from Seattle, security layouts included, but execution's his call."

Molly's boots clicked against the tile as she shifted her weight. "Ana. We both have bosses. We both want this project to succeed. I'd like us to be friends."

Ana studied her for a beat.

"I respect directness," she said finally. "But down here, being sweet gets you further than swinging a hammer. More bees with honey."

Molly stopped pacing. Lowered her hands. "I'm sorry."

Ana nodded. "Apology accepted. Let's start over."

"I'd like that," Molly said, extending her hand. "Molly Monroe."

"Ana Lopez."

"I'm telling you," Ana said later, gesturing toward her empty wineglass, "he's impossible when he's working. But once you get him to sit still..."

Molly narrowed her eyes. "Then what?"

Ana smiled. "You'll see."

They were laughing when Jackson stepped inside, eyebrows lifting at the scene. "If that wine box is any indication, I'm guessing you two are bonding."

"Well, it's after hours," Ana said cheerfully. "Cheers."

"Didn't realize we were hosting happy hour."

That did it. Molly laughed so hard she slid halfway out of her chair.

"Jackson would be fine, Ms. Molly," he said, checking the box. "How long have you been waiting?"

Ana laughed until she hiccupped. Molly laughed until she tipped right out of her chair.

"I'm calling Marco," Jackson said. "Ana, you're not driving."

"Oh," Ana sang. "Someone's in trouble."

Molly pointed, breathless with laughter. "That's you."

Chapter Seven

Jackson

"Hey, Marco." Jackson greeted Ana's husband fifteen minutes later and pointed at his secretary. "I don't know what happened. Figured I'd call instead of letting her drive home."

"Thanks, Jackson. She looks like she's having a good time." He patted his wife's boss on the back and then, with an arm wrapped around Ana, helped her out the door and into their car in the parking lot.

"You're a decent man, Mr. Beaumont. I want to like you," said Molly from the floor.

"Why wouldn't you like me?" he said and sat down in the chair Ana had just vacated.

"You make my job so hard. A ghost! That's what you are. You keep disappearing."

"Hmmm," he reflected. Looking closely at her wild hair and tight jeans. Jackson tipped his head, considering her. "You got my attention now, don't you?"

"I'm drunk!" she said, and smacked the floor before laughing and throwing her head back onto the seat behind her.

"I can see that, but the women I've been working with was much too uptight for that. Look at you in jeans and boots. You look as wild as a newborn filly."

"I don't know what that is..." Dropping her chin to her chest, she lowered her voice and whispered hushed words to him. "Listen...I need this to work." Her words petered off, and she sat there, chin down and eyes closed.

Jackson sighed. "Alright, Ms. Monroe. What desperately required my presence?"

Molly, still sitting on the tiled floor, said, "You are insufferable."

The two sat in silence. Jackson looked around the lobby of the company he'd made. He'd patterned the tiled floors and laid them down himself. The mahogany receptionist's desk was his grandfather's that he'd had refinished early in his career. It was showing signs of age and use, again. Everything was masculine in understated creams and chrome. The only color came from the brick red chairs he and Molly were sharing.

"I know what it's like to fight to win, Ms. Molly, but you can't lose yourself." For a moment he sat waiting for her to reply. When she didn't answer him, he reached over to tap her shoulder. "Are you sleeping?"

"No, I'm thinking."

"You don't seem like the type to go on a bender. What happened with Ana today?"

"Nothing. Ana's wonderful."

"I wouldn't argue that, but..." he gestured to her sitting on the floor, "From the small amount I've learned about you, this looks out of character."

"In the last seventy-two hours, my boyfriend has dumped me, I've been forced to Texas for my job, and my hair has taken on a life of its own. I needed to...do something. Ana offered to help."

Jackson chuckled, then—to her surprise—leaned down and offered his hand.

Molly blinked at him, suspicious. "What are you doing?"

"Making sure you get a proper Texas welcome," he smirked. "Come on. I think we need to get you some food. Ana is an amazing cook, but I'm sure she didn't feed you before y'all started on that box."

"Can we have BBQ? Man, I'd love some fried pickles. Ana says—"

Jackson's rumbling laugh reverberated through the room. "Texas seems to be rubbing off on you, and it didn't take long." Leaning down to put his arms under her, he helped her up from the floor. "Come on. I know a place."

Molly groaned, then said, "Fine."

Sweet Sally's Bayou BBQ sat nestled south of Serenity, tucked between sprawling live oak trees and the warm scent of smoked hickory. Jackson glanced at Molly from the driver's seat, watching as she leaned against the door, her chin resting in her palm. She looked relaxed for the first time since stepping foot in Texas. He hadn't meant to make her chase him down at the office today. He'd known she'd come looking for him eventually—it was just in her nature. Her tenacity was as impressive as it was frustrating.

He cleared his throat and tapped the steering wheel. "It's a bit of a drive, but I figured you could use the time to sober up."

She shot him an indignant look and said, "I'm not that drunk," though the slight slur to her words hinted otherwise.

He smirked. "You're in for a treat. Ms. Sally's been cooking BBQ for over thirty years. I used to come here after football games. She's seen me through birthdays, weddings, even a funeral, or two."

That got her attention. She shifted to face him, her blonde curls a little wilder than usual, and he had to tear his eyes away from the way they framed her face. "I've got a place like that back home—Mama Malone's. I haven't been going there as long, but they still treat me like family."

"Sally's worse than family." He said. "She wants to know all my business, feed me, and then make me pay for the privilege."

Molly's laughter hit him low in his stomach. *Trouble.* She was too easy to like, too easy to look at, and, he suspected, too darn easy to fall for.

"I can't wait to meet her," she said, stretching her arms with a lazy smile.

"Just a few more minutes. How are you feeling?"

She rolled down the window, letting the humid Texas air curl around them. "Wonderful," she said, tilting her head back against the seat. "I've never smelled anything like this before."

Jackson inhaled deeply, filling his lungs with the familiar mix of salt and earth. "The bay meets the bayou here. Salt from the Gulf mixed with the swamp. It's eau de le South."

With a gentle breath, she let the moment wash over her. "It makes me want to walk under the stars. It's been so long since I've seen this many."

He watched the way the street lamps reflected in her blue eyes. "Serenity's close enough to the city but still tucked into nature. Some land out here isn't worth building on, so you get little pockets of wilderness." A small smile tugged at his lips. "But in a second, we'll be back in civilization."

She turned toward him fully now, studying him in a way that made his grip tighten around the wheel. "Will you take me for a walk?"

His fingers twitched, and for a fleeting second, he thought about pulling over right then and there. It wouldn't take much—a few steps into the trees, the soft rustle of leaves beneath their boots. Maybe even his palm resting against the small of her back as he led her somewhere quiet.

Instead, he forced himself to keep his focus on the road, on the glowing neon sign of Sweet Sally's shining just ahead. "Let's get you fed first," he said, pushing every ounce of his charm into a grin.

Because keeping a professional distance? Yeah...that was getting harder by the second.

Jackson held the door open as they stepped into Sweet Sally's Bayou BBQ, the rich scent of smoked and slow-cooked meat enveloping them. He'd been coming here since he was a kid. It was as much home as any other place in Serenity. Tonight, though, he wasn't here for the memories. He was here to make up for being a jackass.

He shouldn't have left her stranded at the Calypso, or forced her to come to his office. Well, he hadn't forced her to get drunk with Ana, but that rest? That was on him. And now, despite his better judgment, he wanted to make her feel like maybe Texas wasn't the worst place in the world to be.

"Ms. Sally! I brought you a convert!" he called out, his voice carrying over the clatter of plates and the hum of conversation.

Behind the counter, an older woman wiped her hands on her apron as she emerged from the kitchen, her gray curls bouncing with every step. "Bless your heart," she said, beaming as she pulled him into a hug. "Boy, come here and give me a hug."

Jackson grinned, bending slightly to wrap his arms around her. "Ma'am, you know I've missed you."

She patted his cheek. "And don't you forget it. You want the usual?"

"Yes, ma'am. Two specials."

"With pleasure." She turned and hollered into the kitchen, "Jeffrey! Two pulled pork plates with all the fixings and a pitcher of sweet tea." Then, glancing past him, she gave Molly an assessing look. "And who's this sweet thing?"

He caught Molly's surprised blink before she recovered, straightening her posture. "A friend," he said before she could fix her mouth to argue. "We're enjoying the evening."

"Well, I'm glad you're enjoying it here."

"There's nowhere else for me, Ms. Sally," said Jackson with a wink, as he guided Molly toward a back booth. She followed, her gaze sweeping the restaurant, enjoying the black-and-white photos on the walls and the inviting charm of the place.

"This place is straight out of a movie,"

Jackson smirked. "Wait until morning. It's too dark to see, but outside those windows is a lake. When the sun comes up, the water catches the light just right. And Ms. Sally makes the best pancakes to go with the view."

She glanced toward the curtained windows, intrigued. "I'd like to see that."

He slid into his seat, watching her as she settled in. "So, Ms. Molly, what brings an uptight woman like you to Texas looking to unwind?"

Her blue eyes flickered with challenge at his teasing, and he couldn't help but admire how she stood her ground. "I'm sure you knew this wasn't part of the plan."

"Oh, absolutely." He smirked. "World domination was, though."

She rolled her eyes, but there was amusement in the motion. "And—"

"Order up!" Ms. Sally interrupted, sliding two heaping plates of food in front of them. "You two be civil with each other," she said, and waved her finger at them before disappearing back into the kitchen.

"Yes, ma'am." Jackson nudged Molly's plate toward her—not that she needed much encouragement. Her eyes widened.

"There's so much food."

"No one leaves Ms. Sally's hungry."

She scanned her plate, then arched a brow at him. "We

didn't order fried pickles."

"Well, I guess that means we'll have to come back."

She didn't even argue. Just picked up her fork and stabbed a thick bite of barbecue, lifting it reverently to her mouth. The moment it touched her tongue, she hummed in appreciation, closing her eyes.

Jackson couldn't help but watch her, drawn in by the sheer satisfaction on her face. It was all he could do not to shift in his seat as she fill her mouth with juicy meat.

Breathe.

He took a slow bite of his own, savoring the same flavors he knew by heart, giving himself a second to rein it in.

When she finally opened her eyes, she wiped her lips with a napkin. "So good," she said, then took another bite.

Amused, he let her eat, watching with something dangerously close to affection. He enjoyed seeing her like this, relaxed, and happily stuffing her face. The sharp edges he saw on the job site softened in the presence of comfort food.

Minutes later, when she finally slowed down, she pointed her fork at him. "You've got me beat. Best place ever."

"Told you."

"I can admit when I'm wrong. Write this down—it doesn't happen often."

His lips twisted. Tipping his head, he said, "I'll cherish the moment."

She settled deeper into the seat, looking more at ease than he'd ever seen her.

"I'm glad you're enjoying it," he said. "It's the least I can do to make up for how much trouble I've caused."

"The words sound like an apology, but the tone sounds sarcastic."

He smirked, leaning back in his seat. "I take my work seriously, Molly. This is as important to me as it is to you." He fiddled with his fork before turning his attention back to her. "Your story?"

She paused, then lowered her gaze to her plate, stabbing at her coleslaw like she was debating her next words. Her usual confidence flickered, replaced by something hesitant.

"I grew up in Seattle," she finally said. "Just outside a little suburb called Shoreline. Have you been to Washington state?"

"No, can't say I have."

The corners of her lips lifted slightly. "It's all mountains and trees along the coastline, mixed with salty ocean water and lakes everywhere. Inland, on the other side of the mountains, it's desert dry, and you can watch the tumbleweeds roll across the roads."

Jackson tilted his head. "Sounds a little like Texas."

She said, shaking her head. "Not even close. This place is something all its own." Molly speared another bite, and chewed before finishing what she was saying, "My mom was a stay-at-home mom. My dad worked a lot. I was an only child, so they had plenty of time to focus on me, but it never felt like enough. I didn't realize until I was older—my mom was depressed, and my dad was cheating. They separated when I was in high school." Her eyes flicked up to his. "I won't depend on anyone to take care of me."

He nodded, something about the confession settling deep in his chest. "You look like you're doing a stand-up job looking out for yourself. We'll overlook this evening," he said, trying to draw a smile out of her.

She huffed a laugh, shaking her head. "I'm so full. I need to get back to my hotel. The guy in charge of my project is a lunatic and shows up at six in the morning."

He let out a soft laugh, but a heaviness from her words stayed with him. Maybe it was knowing she wouldn't be here forever. Maybe it was knowing he was part of why she kept running herself ragged.

"Sounds like I'd best get you back to your car," he said, offering her a small smile, but it almost felt like she didn't want to leave, either.

Chapter Eight

Jackson

After paying the tab and saying goodbye to Ms. Sally, Jackson led Molly out into the dimly lit gravel parking lot. He opened the passenger door of his truck, slid the to-go boxes onto the bench seat, and turned back toward her.

He'd spent half the night trying to remind himself why it was important to keep her far away. She was only here for her job. Once that was done, she'd be gone, but Molly Monroe had a way of sinking her teeth into things, whether it was a project, an argument—or him.

She had every right to be angry with having to hunt him down. That was on him, but he hadn't expected her to show up, guns blazing, demanding answers like a five-foot-four force of nature. Now, under the Southern night sky, he felt the pull of her presence.

Jackson leaned against the open door, arms crossed. "I know you said you needed to get back, but earlier, you mentioned a walk. There's a little path that runs around the lake. We could follow it for a bit."

Molly hesitated, glancing at the open truck cab before looking back at him. He could see the gears turning in her head. She was weighing her options, deciding if a moonlit walk with him was a bad idea. She was sobering up, but he was still hoping she'd say yes.

Finally, she smiled, soft and a little teasing. "What harm could a little moonlight walk do?"

Jackson pushed the door shut with a click and held out his hand. "Wouldn't want you to trip in the dark."

"You're just making sure I don't get hurt so they don't send you someone worse than me to finish this project.," she said, but she placed her hand in his anyway. Lord help him. Her hand felt small in his. It was tiny, but surprisingly steady.

"Is that possible?"

He led her to a narrow break in the trees, guiding her through the dark with slow steps. The Texas air was warm, thick with the scent of briny water. The quiet wrapped around them like a well-worn quilt, the cicadas and the distant hum of Sweet Sally's jukebox filling the silence between them.

"Probably not."

Jackson felt a shift. It wasn't just the night, or the air. It was her. Molly Monroe, despite her high-powered job and polished appearance, felt like she fit here. Like she belonged next to him, walking down this dirt path instead of in a skyscraper with city lights outside her window.

"This way," he said, leading her through the opening in the trees. "It'll be dark at first, but the trees open up by the water." As they stepped into a clearing, the moon cast a silver sheen over the rippling surface of the lake.

"It's beautiful," she said.

"Back in high school, the guys and I used to bring dates out here to make out."

She smirked. "Dropping hints?"

He chuckled. "Saving those for the second date."

She laughed at that, a soft, genuine sound. "A second date? You're confident, aren't you?"

Jackson shot her a sideways grin. "I know a good thing when I see it."

Before she could respond, a shuffle in the nearby brush startled her. She jumped, bumping into him.

"What was that?"

Jackson tightened his grip on her hand. "Probably an armadillo. Maybe a possum."

She tensed slightly before exhaling. He could feel her body relax against his. "I can't remember the last time I was out this late at night."

"Me neither. Working early means I'm usually in bed by now."

She let out a thoughtful hum. "I probably should have done this instead of drinking. There's something peaceful about being in the dark where no one can see you."

His chest tightened at the truth beneath her words. "Are you worried about being seen?"

She hesitated. "Aren't *you*?"

He thought about that. "Sometimes."

The distant buzz of the bar's jukebox drifted through the trees, filling the silence.

Molly sighed, her voice softer now. "It's rough being a woman in business. Feels like I have to work twice as hard to be taken seriously."

Jackson watched her. He admired the way she stood tall despite everything. She'd shown him that when she'd showed up at his office. Molly was determined to win and unwilling to back down. It was an appealing trait. It meant she wouldn't disappear at the first sign of trouble.

Behind them, a car rumbled to life in the parking lot, bringing them both back to reality. She straightened, squeezing his hand briefly and muttering. "I should get back. Thank you for my moonlit walk."

"Anytime," Jackson said, pulling her hand a little closer before releasing it.

As they turned back toward the truck, Jackson realized something: *he wanted her to stay.* The project, the business, the whole stupid professional distance thing—none of it mattered in this moment. All he wanted was to stay here, hidden in the dark, with Molly Monroe.

The drive back to Jackson's office was quiet. She sat beside him, the to-go carton resting in her lap, and the smell of barbecue lingering in the air.

A soft breeze whistled through the cracked window as the city lights grew brighter in the distance.

"I've just noticed something," she murmured.

"What's that?" Jackson asked, keeping his eyes on the road

but feeling the weight of her gaze on him.

"Everything out here is so flat. There aren't any hills like there are in Seattle. If it wasn't for all the trees and bushes, you could probably see for miles. The ground would be a field of stars at night."

He glanced at her before turning his attention back to the highway. "Maybe, when this project's done, I'll take you to the hill country."

She turned slightly toward him, as if picturing it.

"Maybe," she whispered. Something about the way she said it made him wish for more.

He pulled into the gravel lot outside his office, the building dark now, the job trailers quiet. Suddenly the world felt too big again. Too bright. Too much space between them.

"Here we are," he said, putting the truck in park.

"Thanks for driving," she murmured.

He huffed a quiet laugh.

"Okay," she added, lifting a brow. "Ignoring the fact that I definitely couldn't drive earlier."

"It was my pleasure."

"I'm still not used to driving out here. Everything's so dark and flat—I keep feeling like I'm going to miss a turn and end up in another county."

His grip on the steering wheel tightened, then loosened. He turned to her, eyes steady. "Then let me pick you up in the morning. Save you the stress."

She hesitated. "You don't have to do that. I'll figure it out."Jackson's lips quirked up in a slow, knowing smirk. "I don't mind."She exhaled, glancing at him before nodding.

"That...would actually be nice. Thank you."

"Or maybe you're agreeing just to make sure I actually show up," he said lightly. "I will."

Molly gave him a little side-eye and a laugh. "Perhaps."

"Be ready at six-thirty. We can show up a little late since I know the boss."

"Oh, good! I can sleep in."

He grinned. "At least we'll know we'll be on site together. You won't have to stage another elaborate espionage mission to hunt me down."

"Sounds like a plan."

Molly reached for the door handle, glancing toward her car parked a few spaces down, but before she could hop out, he moved.

He opened his door and was outside in an instant, rounding the truck to her side, opening her door before she could protest. Then, he reached out a hand to help her down from the truck.

"I had a lovely time this evening, Ms. Molly. Thanks for keeping me company."

As she shifted closer, the heat of his body pressed into hers for half a second longer than necessary. He caught the way she exhaled, just barely, her lips parting slightly. Her breath, warm and hesitant, brushed against his neck.

Then, instead of closing the space, he pulled back.

He placed the to-go container in her hands instead. "Wouldn't want Ms. Sally thinking I let you go hungry."

She licked her lips, blinking up at him before nodding. "Thank you."

"Night, Molly."

She walked away, and Jackson exhaled slowly before heading back to his truck.

"This might be a problem," he said into the night air.

Chapter Nine

Molly

The phone ringing jolted Molly awake.

"Good morning! This is the front desk. You have a visitor. Would you like me to send him up?"

"Uh, no. Tell him I'll be right down."

As she brushed the sleep out of her eyes and ran her fingers through her knotted hair. "Slept in, Molly? Seriously?"

She half-rolled, half-flopped out of bed, snagging yesterday's jeans off the floor on her way back up. One leg at a time, she hopped around the hotel room, pulling them on while chugging the hotel's overpriced bottled water from the nightstand. She slipped into her bra as she shuffled towards the mirror.

A quick swipe of lip gloss and mascara would have to do. She thanked her mother's genetics for halfway decent skin, took one last breath, and headed out the door five minutes later. Straightening her top and pulling her hair back in the cramped elevator had been a challenge, but somehow, it worked. Almost composed, she faced the opening doors with a deep breath and a shaky smile.

"Good morning," Jackson was waiting for her in the lobby, already holding out a to-go cup. "I thought you'd forgotten."

"What?" She raised a brow, accepting the coffee with a grateful sigh. "I've been up waiting for you."

"You're a terrible liar this early in the morning."

When she took her first sip, a moan of appreciation escaped before she could stop it.

Jackson smirked. "I'm going to have to keep feeding you."

She winked at him over the rim of her cup, but didn't stop drinking.

"You ready?"

Sufficiently caffeinated, she nodded. "Okay, lead the way."

Molly watched the landscape blur past the truck window as Jackson expertly navigated Serenity's back roads, taking the fastest route to the job site. She cradled the warm coffee cup in her hands, letting the heat seep into her fingers. Was it just the coffee warming her belly that morning? Or, Perhaps it was last night's lingering memory of Jackson's slow drawl, and his hand warm in hers during their walk.

"I owe you an apology for last night." Molly traced her thumb over the seam of her jeans.

Jackson's hands tightened on the steering wheel, just enough to make the leather creak. "Oh?" He drawled.

She caught the way his eyes flickered toward her, just for a second, and swallowed before she said, "Yeah, that...isn't how I typically introduce myself to our contractors." She forced a small, half-hearted laugh, but the warmth creeping up her neck betrayed her.

He let out a low chuckle, deep and familiar. "I didn't think it was." Jackson turned, his profile sharp against the morning light. "I did like our walk, though."

"Me, too."

"You don't regret it, do you?"

Molly inhaled, slow and steady. Did she regret it? The hush of the lake, the cicadas humming beneath a dark velvety sky. Or the way she had felt like melting into him?

"No," she admitted softly, before she could stop herself. "I don't think I could if I wanted to."

She shifted in her seat, glancing out the window—anywhere but at him. What had gotten into her? She was practical. Focused. She had spent years structuring her life down to the hour, timing every move toward success. And yet...

Her thoughts drifted back to the night before—the quiet walk, the way the world had gone still around them, the look in Jackson's eyes when she'd finally let her guard slip. It could have gone differently.

She pressed a hand to her coffee cup, grounding herself. *He's your employee. You don't live here. Keep it simple.*

Jackson exhaled sharply beside her, as if he could sense the storm of thoughts she was fighting. His fingers tapped a steady rhythm on the gearshift. "Good," he said, his voice even, breaking the quiet.

Molly forced her gaze forward, focusing on the steady hum of tires on pavement. How was she supposed to step out of his truck and pretend that nothing had changed?

He looked perfectly at ease, one hand on the steering wheel, sunlight catching in his hair, as if last night hadn't altered the space between them at all. As if he hadn't unsettled her simply by caring when she least expected it.

She took another sip of coffee, willing herself to calm. She could handle this. She had to.

"Hey, Boss," Duncan greeted as they arrived. "Ms. Molly," he said, and handed her a hard hat. It was bright pink.

"Uh, thanks?" She held the hat awkwardly in her hands.

"Put it on!" Duncan grinned. "The guys figured you should have a hat of your own, since you'll be spending more time here. No need to keep wearing whatever some sweaty guy had on his head last."

Molly's lips twitched, and with renewed enthusiasm, she said, "Tell the guys I said thanks, Duncan." She settled the hat on her head, adjusting the strap against her hair.

"That was thoughtful of you," Jackson said, looking closer at Duncan.

Duncan tipped his own hat with a wink, and said, "He's not used to anyone thinking of things before he does." Then he walked off, leaving Molly laughing.

Jackson huffed. "Let's gather the crew."

"Admit it. He's got game even if he is as old as my dad."

"I just don't get why he's playing." Jackson shoved his hands in his pockets, pivoted on his boots, and strode toward the hotel entrance. "Let's look around while he pulls everyone together." He held the battered front door open for her while she entered.

Molly walked past the boarded-up windows and imagined what they'd looked like before being sealed with sun bleached gray wood and spray paint. Jackson propped the doors open and joined her in the lobby next to the water warped remains of the check-in desk.

"I can't believe this will become what Paul and Mr. Maherson envision," Molly admitted. She could see some progress. There were large black bags piled in a corner and the loose debris that had littered the lobby on her tour with Duncan seemed more under control. The once-grand hotel was being unearthed from beneath years of neglect, but it wasn't enough. "It's like they're asking you to turn a cardboard box into a yacht."

"With money and time, anything's possible."

"True, but we're on a time line and a tight budget." Pausing by one of the grimy lobby windows, she peered out at the men gathering next to Duncan. "The grounds are looking way better."

"It's amazing what determined hands and some focused labor can accomplish,"

"I can't believe how much has changed in just a few days. There's still work to be done making it guest ready, but the garbage is cleared, the overgrown landscaping is under control, and the pool actually looks like a pool. Can you believe Duncan says they'll be moving inside tomorrow?"

"Right on schedule," Jackson said with no small satisfaction. "Once the interior is gutted, which will take about a week, we can start rebuilding."

"Have you looked at the designers' reports?" Molly wandered over to a pile of discarded curtains, nudging at them with her shoe.

A rat scurried out.

She shrieked, stumbling backward—right into the remains of a broken armchair. The unexpected movement sent her tumbling to the ground with a sharp jolt to her ankle.

"Molly!" Jackson was at her side in an instant. "Tell me where it hurts."

"My butt and my ego aren't doing so great, but most of the pain is here." She winced, pressing a hand to her throbbing foot.

"Boss? What happened?" Duncan rushed inside. "I heard a yell." When his eyes landed on Molly, he asked, "Should I call 9-1-1?"

"No, I think she's okay, but she twisted her ankle. I'm going to take her to see Jessica at the clinic," said Jackson, then he tossed his keys to Duncan. "Can you bring my truck around near the door?"

Molly tried to get up and winced. "Jessica, huh? You have a person for everything, don't you?"

"She and I...we go back." Jackson shrugged.

"An ex, huh? I'd rather go someplace else."

"And sit for hours waiting?"

"Well, when you put it like that."

"Hold on," he said. In one swift motion, Jackson scooped her up. A soft whimper escaped her lips; his grip shifted. "Did I hurt you?"

"Just a little."

His lips were two thin lines, and they'd lost all their color. His jaw tightened. "Careful now," he said, as he carefully carried Molly to his truck. "Duncan, take care of the crew. No one else gets hurt today. Pay overtime if you have to."

"Yes, sir. Take good care of Ms. Monroe."

"I will." Jackson could hear Duncan giving orders to the crew as Jackson settled Molly into his truck. He looked at her and said, "I'm going to make this better, I promise."

Chapter Ten

Jackson

Jackson ran a hand through his hair, exhaling as he paced the clinic lobby. *This is my fault.* His gut twisted as he glanced toward the patient area.

He never should've let her go inside the hotel. He should've insisted the crew clear every hazard first—refused to let her step foot in there before he made it safe.

"Well, her pulse is elevated, and her color's a little off. Definite signs of stress," Jessica said, watching him pace. "We're waiting on the X-rays, but will have them soon."

He knew better. He could have called it from the first moment he saw her in those stupid high heels stumbling in the parking lot. She wasn't weak. Hell, she fought him at every turn, but that didn't change the fact that she wasn't used to this kind of work. Business meetings didn't involve loose floorboards and rat infestations. She might be as stubborn as a mule, but she wasn't indestructible.

"Thanks, Jess," he said, rubbing his palms against his jeans.

Jessica looked at him, curious. "At some point, Jack, you have to stop calling in freebies."

"Hey! I helped build this place. If I recall, you were pretty happy with 'free' back then."

"Hush. We'll stick to our usual arrangement." She said, swatting his shoulder with her clipboard. "You owe me next time I need help here."

Her teasing didn't ease the tightness in his chest. It made it worse. Because Molly didn't have anyone else looking out for her. He was the only one.

"Can I go see her now?"

Jessica nodded. "She's been asking for you."

Something hot and unsteady curled in his stomach at that.

When they reached the exam room, he knocked lightly. A muffled response came from within. He spotted her when he stepped into the room. She was lounging on the exam table in a pair of hospital scrub bottoms, her cheeks still flushed from whatever medication Jess had given her.

She looked small. Too delicate. Too out of place. *What was I thinking?*

Then, she looked up at him. *Grinned.* "You look like you're feeling better," he said, walking over.

"I could get used to this treatment. Top-tier meds, stylish pajama pants, and the fastest service I've ever had." Her voice was looser, lighter. "You must be really close with Dr. Louis."

The lingering warmth of her words sent a sharp pang through his chest. He wanted it to mean something, and it did. *Maybe.* If she wasn't drunk smiling at him, she was high. How would she feel about him when she was stone cold sober?

"She's a good friend."

Molly hummed, tilting her head. "Do you stay friends with all your exes?"

"What did she say?" His smile faded.

"Meh. She was mostly complaining about you. Answer my question."

"Not always," he admitted, then winced. He didn't want to lie to Molly, but he wasn't about to unpack his personal life with his ex in her exam room. Instead, Jackson latched onto the easiest distraction and nodded toward her relaxed posture. "How are those pain pills?"

She ran her hands down her face, stretching the soft skin of her cheeks and eyes until she looked ridiculous. Then, with the most exaggerated flourish, she beamed.

"Never mind," he said, shaking his head.

The door swung open again, and Jessica reappeared, holding a chart close to her chest. "Good call bringing her in, Jack. It's not badly broken, but there is a small fracture. She'll need a walking boot and a week, or two, off her feet. The swelling needs time to go down before we consider any follow up treatment."

Jackson exhaled, relief taking the edge off his nerves.

Molly, however, was all enthusiasm. "It doesn't hurt. I feel wonderful! Just take me back to my hotel, and I'll be on-site tomorrow."

Jackson restrained a groan.

"That's the meds talking," he said. "She'll be the death of me. Jess, what did you give her?"

Jessica grinned. "She'll sober up in a few hours. I'll send her with a prescription for something milder." Her gaze flicked to

Jackson, something not quite teasing in her smirk. "After that, Tylenol is fine, but the best treatment is to stay off of it."

Jackson knew how well that would go. "I'm not sure she'll be capable of doing that."

"Well, I'm sure you can find a way to keep your girlfriend off her feet." Jessica tipped her head.

Jackson choked. "She's not—"

"Hmm." Jessica smirked. "However you define it, she needs rest. I'll leave you two to talk about it. You can check-out with Beth at the front desk. See ya around, Jackson."

The second Jessica left, he turned to Molly. "Alright, let's get—"

She'd snuggled against the pillow, body curled around it like a contented cat, and a soft snore escaped her lips.

Jackson sighed and said, "Molly?"

Nothing.

He tapped the side of the bed. "Come on, darlin'. Wake up."

She made a sleepy noise of protest, half mumbling, "Bed." Then she rolled onto her back, sending the exam room paper crinkling beneath her.

Lord, he was in trouble. He dragged a hand down his face, muttered a quick prayer, and made his way to the front desk. She was still out when he came back. *Stubborn as hell,* he thought, before carefully adjusting her leg and the walking boot.

She stirred.

With excruciating gentleness, he eased his arms under her and gathered her against his chest. This close, he could smell the light scent of her shampoo, could feel the subtle way she automatically curled in toward his warmth.

A protective instinct curled deep inside him. She was alone in Texas. No family. No backup plan. *And she's hurt because I didn't keep her safe.*

As he carried her out to his truck, he made a quiet promise to himself.

Next time, she wouldn't have to ask for him.

Next time, he'd already be there.

Chapter Eleven

Molly

When she woke up, she was in a massive bedroom, and nestled in a huge four-poster bed made of sturdy oak. A sturdy dresser stood against the far wall with matching nightstands on both sides of the bed. A plush cream-colored rug covered the floor. To her left, a fireplace crackled beside a small seating area, casting a warm glow across the room. Faint music played somewhere beyond the closed door.

"Hello?" she called, shifting to sit up. The movement sent a sharp jolt of pain through her ankle, and she gasped. When she pulled back the blankets, she found a thick black brace securing her foot. Its weight pressed against her leg. The sight of hospital scrubs jolted her muddled thoughts, and fragments of memory fell into place.

"Jackson?" She tried again, louder this time.

The bedroom door creaked open moments later, and Ana peeked her head inside. "Hey, you're awake."

"Ana? Is this your house?"

Ana let out a short laugh as she stepped into the room. "Only if Jackson suddenly decided to pay me a lot more." She walked over and sat on the bed. "This is his place. He had some jobs to check on and wanted to make sure the Calypso crew was settling in, since he didn't get to talk to them much this morning. How are you feeling? Do you need more medicine?"

"I never want to take that stuff, again. God, I can't even imagine the nonsense I must've said." She shook her head, resting her hand on her forehead.

Ana patted her knee. "How about food instead? I brought some of my abuela's pork tamales. She made them fresh this morning."

When her stomach growled, Molly said, "That sounds amazing. I could eat a whole pig."

Ana grinned. "I'll remember that when we throw our next big pit BBQ."

"So, Jackson roped you into babysitting me, huh? Why didn't he take me back to my hotel?"

Ana scoffed. "Have you met him? There's no way he was sending you back there to recover alone. And judging by the list of things he left for me before he took off, I think you might live here now."

She blinked. "Excuse me?"

Molly barely had time to process Ana's amused expression before the sound of the front door clicking shut sent her heart skittering. Footsteps approached, steady and familiar, and she swallowed hard, bracing herself.

"Jackson?" Ana called, twisting toward the doorway. "She's awake. We're up here!"

Molly pressed her palms into the blankets and sat up, shifting carefully to avoid jarring her ankle. Heat prickled through her as she thought about what it meant that she was lying in his bed instead of a sterile hotel room. Of all the places she expected to wake up, it hadn't been here.

Ana shot her a knowing look, murmuring, "I'll let him explain."

Molly scowled. "Scaredy-cat."

Seconds later, Jackson filled the doorway, his tall frame filling up the surrounding space. He nodded toward Ana. His voice was as calm as ever. "Thanks, Ana. I know you need to get back to Marco. Can you stop by tomorrow? I'll text you the time."

Ana smirked as she waggled her fingers in a silent 'call me' gesture before slipping past him. Molly's stomach dipped, nerves twisting into something she couldn't name. When the door clicked shut behind Ana, a quiet hush settled over the room, wrapping between them.

Jackson exhaled and pressed his hands against the door frame.

Molly folded her arms. "You don't have to keep me here, you know."

He nodded, stepping farther inside. "I know." His voice was calm, unreadable. He watched her, assessing how much pain she might be in. "But, I'd like you to stay."

Something inside her clenched. She had spent so much time proving she didn't need anyone. But she wasn't in Seattle anymore, and if she was honest with herself, the idea of going back to her silent hotel room, swallowing painkillers and forcing herself to limp to the bathroom, made her chest feel tight.

She tugged at the blanket and twisted her fingers into the fabric before shaking her head. "Honestly, Jackson, I appreciate the offer, but it's unnecessary."

He sat on the bed, his knee brushing the mattress. "Who's going to help you at the hotel?" His tone was light, but there was something unwavering beneath it.

"Presumably, the concierge." She scoffed. "That is their job."

Jackson arched an eyebrow. "And if you wake up in the middle of the night and need your medicine? Or, just as likely, you need to go to the bathroom"

Molly hesitated. "I'll still need to go to the bathroom here."

"I can help you."

"So, I'm choosing between my contractor or a stranger helping me pee."

"I think I'm more than a stranger." His voice softened. "Who's going to help you when you need to change?"

Her fingers clenched the blankets tighter.

She was normally so careful about how she presented herself, so meticulous about looking polished and capable. Imagining trying to wrestle herself into anything besides leggings was enough to make her wince.

She swallowed before muttering, "Room service exists...housekeeping...lots of things exist, Jackson."

His brow furrowed, but before he could speak again, his expression shifted.

Something sparked in his eyes, as if he had a sudden realization. "Ana can help you."

Molly let out an exasperated laugh, more at herself than him. Jackson Beaumont was offering to take care of her, and her first instinct was to argue.

"I don't think Ana putting my pants on for me is enough reason to stay."

Jackson settled his weight back onto the bed.

She could see the tension behind his eyes, something unspoken making his jaw tick.

"It's only for a little while," he said. "Jessica—Dr. Louis—said you need at least a week, maybe two."

Her eyebrows lifted. "Two weeks? Jackson, I'm supposed to go back to Seattle in two days!"

He shrugged. "Can't you tell Maherson you need to stay? In a few days, we'll moved to the interior phase. I could use your help with design choices."

She narrowed her eyes. "You fight dirty."

A small, knowing smirk ghosted across his lips. "Is it working?"

Molly's eyelids drooped as she tried to focus. She wasn't used to anyone taking care of her. *Not like this.* What unsettled her more—the offer, or that she wanted to say *yes*?

But what was the alternative? Going back to her hotel room alone would hurt more than her healing ankle. Still...she had to ask, "Why is this so important to you?"

Jackson's mouth opened, then closed. When he finally spoke, he looked away. "I feel bad I didn't keep you safe."

Molly felt her pulse skip. "Jackson, that's *not* your job."

"Yes. Yes, it is." He furrowed his brow. His voice was soft, but firm. "On the job site it is."

She looked at him. "So, if I'd been hurt at my hotel instead, you'd be okay with leaving me on my own?"

His gaze locked onto hers, dark and unwavering. "No." He exhaled roughly. "No, I'd still want to help you."

Her heart clenched. She was foolish to let him take care of her—to let herself get used to something she couldn't have. Instinctively, she reached out. Her fingers landed inches from his knee. "We work together. You can't do this because...well...because you *like* me."

A slow smile tugged at his lips. "That's stupid. We're adults, and I do like you," he admitted. "But, women, you're stubborn."

Her jaw tensed as she glanced down at her lap.

"I can't mess this job up."

"We're going to make the Calypso amazing." Said Jackson. He pointed to the door. "You'll be up and moving in no time. Why do you think you can't do your job from here?"

"My boss doesn't even see me." She leaned back into the pillow, her voice barely audible. "I've tried everything to get his attention."

Jackson said, speaking just as quietly.

"If they don't see you, then they must be blind." The fireplace popped, casting a flickering warmth against the walls. Jackson clenched his hands together, elbows braced against his thighs.

Molly sighed, shifting slightly, only to wince as pain shot up her calf.

Jackson was at her side instantly, hands hovering like she might shatter.

"You're different," he said. "I don't know why, but I want to." He hesitated before rubbing the back of his neck, looking as if he wasn't used to his own honesty. "You're hurt, and I just—" He exhaled heavily. "I thought about you all day. I should have been looking for ways to get rid of you, but I found myself counting down until I could come home."

Molly swallowed hard. "You don't make things easy, do you?" she said, forcing a weak chuckle.

His lips quirked into something that wasn't quite a smile. "Neither do you."

Exasperated, she shook her head, groaning. "Touché." She let out a breath, willing herself to relax. Knowing she was making a choice that would lead exactly where she wasn't supposed to go. "Fine," she said, shifting her weight on the mattress. "You win."

A victorious smile stretched across his face.

"For one week," she said, lifting an eyebrow. "And no funny business."

Jackson held up his hands in mock surrender. "Scout's honor."

At that, she snorted. Then, shifting uncomfortably again, she sighed. "Now, help me to the bathroom," She watched as warmth flooded his face, amusement twinkling behind his guarded expression.

"Anything for you, darlin'."

Chapter Twelve

Molly

"So, does he snore when he sleeps?" Ana as she pushed open the front door with her hip.

Molly, curled up on the camel-colored leather couch, turned her head with a groggy glare. "How the hell would I know?"

"Right, play dumb." Ana winked and handed her a paper cup of coffee with a flourish.

Molly took it with an appreciative sigh. "You're an angel sent from heaven." The warmth seeped through the cup, settling into her fingers, and she took a cautious sip, grateful for the creamy sweetness.

Ana perched on the edge of a recliner, eager for more details. "It doesn't take much to make you happy, does it?"

"If it's creamy, sweet, and has caffeine, I'm in."

Ana smirked but pressed on. "So, how'd it really go last night?"

Molly shifted her injured foot, propping it back up onto a

pillow. The ache remained, but the sharp pain had dulled to a manageable level. She glanced around the living room—masculine, filled with warm, earthy tones and furniture that looked lived in. It felt...natural. Too natural. That was the part that unnerved her.

"Nothing happened. Honest," she said, though there was a hint of something in her voice—maybe disappointment? She pushed the thought aside. "He's a total gentleman. He took the guest bedroom and gave me his bed. It made sense because of the easier access to the bathroom." Molly said, but her lips softened into an unwilling smile. "That guy thinks of everything."

"That's sort of his superpower." Ana settled deeper into the chair, looking at ease.

Molly hummed in agreement and pulled the blanket around her shoulders. "What's his story?"

"No perfect." Ana's brows rose, but she shrugged. "But, also not mine to tell. I can say he's a wonderful boss."

Molly studied her for a moment. Ana was fiercely loyal to him. While she respected the secrecy, it didn't stop her from wanting to know. "Naturally. He must hand out fabulous Christmas gifts."

Ana laughed and nodded. "The best!"

They worked through the day with the kind of ease that comes from mutual understanding—no pressure, no expectations. Ana made calls, sorted papers, and brought snacks, while Molly helped where she could. By late afternoon, the sky outside had deepened to gold, and the house smelled faintly of coffee and printer ink.

When Jackson arrived that evening, he was carrying a big bag of takeout and a stack of job site photos. Molly glanced up from the couch, her heart skipping before she could remind herself to keep things in perspective. This was temporary. He was temporary.

"How'd you and Ana do today?" he asked, setting the food down on the kitchen counter.

"Really well! I like her," she said, watching as he portioned their meal onto plates. "Thanks for letting her keep me company."

Jackson smirked. "She's still getting everything done. While you were napping, she sent me the profit reports on another project and convinced a new client to pay their bill. I don't want you to feel bad that she's here."

"She got everything done?" Molly said, shaking her head. "While I was napping?"

Jackson handed her a plate. "We didn't want to wake you up."

The ease in his voice, the way he said it so casually, made warmth curl in her chest. Could someone want to come home to her? Mitchell had never cared about something as small as letting her sleep. If anything, he'd resented her exhaustion. Molly peeled back another layer of hesitation, letting herself acknowledge the truth—she liked that Jackson wanted to come home to her.

But that was dangerous thinking.

Work was still her focus. It had to be.

"I'll see if I can help more tomorrow." She stretched her shoulders, forcing herself to shake the thought loose.

Jackson nodded. "I bet she'd like that. Just don't start drinking halfway through the day."

"You're not going to let me live that down, are you?"

"Didn't your mom ever teach you about first impressions?"

Molly stiffened, the shift in her expression so immediate that Jackson caught it instantly. Her grip on the plate tightened.

"I'd rather not talk about my mom."

The energy between them shifted. Jackson's smirk faded. His hand jerked as he reached for a fork, knocking a spoon off the counter. It landed with a clatter. "There's a story there," he said, his voice softer now.

"There is."

Jackson scooped up the fallen spoon, setting it in the sink. Then, carefully, he picked up their plates and moved to the coffee table.

"She died when I was seventeen."

Jackson exhaled. "I can't imagine how hard that must've been. For a kid..."

"It was worse watching life fall apart before it even happened," she admitted, her voice tighter than she would have liked. She had mastered keeping her emotions in check over the years. But this? He made her vulnerable and raw. He was dangerous. "By the time it happened, my parents weren't even speaking anymore. My dad couldn't handle it. He left halfway through her chemo treatments. And my mom? She never got over it. Not really."

Jackson stayed quiet, watching her, his attention unwavering.

"For years, it felt like we were holding out for something, some hope that things would turn around." She let out a dry, humorless laugh. "That's probably why I'm like this. It was always, 'Just hold on a little longer, Molly. Be patient. Things will get better.' But they didn't. When she gave up, I had to make them better on my own."

Jackson's gaze softened. "Is that what made you so determined to be tough?"

Molly forced a small smile, pushing past the unexpected tightness in her chest. "You're reading too much into my actions, Mr. Mystery. Why don't you tell me a little about you?"

Jackson studied her, leaned back, stretching an arm across the back of the couch. "I guess I'm the typical rags-to-riches story. Raised by a single mom, no idea who my father was. My ma always says I saved her life because things changed once she had an 'us' instead of only a her."

Molly tilted her head, curious. "So, you never had a dad?"

"I do now. The best one in the world—I just didn't have him right away." Jackson shifted, his hand resting on the knee nearest to her. "My mom married him when I was twelve. The poor guy put up with me breaking the law and tearing up hell, but he stuck around. He was patient and encouraging. Part of the reason I work so hard is to make him proud. If he thinks I'm doing all right, it can't be half bad."

Molly traced the rim of her cup, considering his words. How different would she be with that kind of support growing up? Someone who stayed, no matter what?

The sun was setting outside the living room window, casting long shadows across the space. Jackson pulled out a box of matches and lit a three-wick candle on the coffee table, the warm glow flickering between them.

Molly hesitated, unsure of what to say.

"Do you mind?" he asked, gesturing toward the candle.

"No, it's relaxing," she said. "Thank you."

"I like sitting here when it's peaceful in the evenings," Jackson said. "Construction is never quiet."

Molly allowed herself to sink further into the couch. "I can only imagine. How was work today?"

"Duncan got the lobby cleared. They're moving to the lower levels tomorrow. Some materials are being picked up by Habitat for Humanity."

Molly perked up. "Why would they want all that junk?"

"There's a lot that's still usable—beds, furniture, doors, hardware, tile, light fixtures. Even things like linens and ironing boards. They resell them or use them in their projects."

"Better than everything ending up in the trash."

"Oh, for sure." Jackson reached out, wrapping a finger around one of her curls, letting it slide through his fingers. It was such a simple gesture, but the intimacy in it sent a slow, simmering heat through her chest. His eyes flickered to her ankle. "Are you feeling better today?"

She hesitated, hyper-aware of how comfortable this moment felt. It was unnerving how easy it was to fall into step with him. "The ankle is still achy. As long as I don't move too quickly, the sharp pain stays at bay."

"I'm so sorry you got hurt," Jackson said, his voice tight with frustration. "I shouldn't have let you in there until it was cleared." His fingers flexed before he dropped his hands to his lap.

"Excuse me?" Molly arched a brow. "May I remind you I'm a grown-ass woman?"

Jackson said with a laugh, "I'm not sure you'd let me forget."

The warmth between them lingered, but something changed—an unspoken shift, like the edges of something fraying.

Molly twisted the blanket in her lap, while Jackson busied himself with clearing their plates. When he leaned over to blow out the candle, she cleared her throat. "I think I'm ready for bed."

Jackson hesitated a moment, then nodded. "Me too." He turned back to her. "Carry you up?"

Her frustration faded. She liked this part too much. The way his arms felt wrapped around her and his breath fanning against her cheek as he lifted her effortlessly. The way he didn't seem to mind taking care of her.

"Yes," she said, hoping her voice wouldn't crack. She wrapped her arms around his neck, her body molding against his. Her fingers played at the edge of his collar, resisting the urge to run through his hair.

"Were you warm enough last night?" he asked, his voice full of something she couldn't quite name.

"Yeah." Her words were quiet, only a whisper. Her fingers squeezed his shoulders. She shouldn't be indulging in this. She shouldn't be letting herself fall.

And yet.

She exhaled against his neck, letting her lips brush the small, soft place behind his ear. Jackson's breath caught.

Turning sideways to carry her through the bedroom door, he moved to the bed and lowered her onto the turned-down sheets. "You know you can call me if you need anything, right?"

She hesitated, the weight of everything settling between them.

He was letting her in. She could see it. Feel it.

And God help her—she was letting him in, too.

"Yes," she whispered.

She watched as he turned. He hesitated at the door. "Molly."

"Yeah?"

He exhaled. "Goodnight."

She swallowed. "Goodnight."

Goodnights turned into mornings, and mornings into something that felt dangerously like a pattern.

Jackson's presence threaded itself into her days—coffee waiting on the counter, the low murmur of his voice on early calls, the quiet way he made space for her without ever asking for anything in return.

Ana dropped by most afternoons, bright and talkative, filling the house with the clatter of dishes and her relentless curiosity. When Molly teased her about getting paid time and a half to babysit, Ana had only grinned. "Worth every penny."

The joke had landed softly, but the realization hadn't. Jackson wasn't just kind—he was hopelessly selfless. Everything he did carried an easy generosity, the kind that expected nothing back. And she was falling for it. For him.

Every evening, like clockwork, he came through the door carrying the weight of his day on broad shoulders, only to shrug it off with that slow, crooked grin. He always found her first. Sometimes with a teasing comment about her monopolizing his couch, sometimes with a brief, casual touch that lingered longer than it should have. The familiarity was equal parts comfort and danger.

Nights were the hardest. When the sun sank and the world went quiet, it was just the two of them. The chemistry was easy, unguarded, and comfortable. In those hours, she almost forgot who she was supposed to be.

But the guilt always followed. Her work still mattered—more than mattered. It was the culmination of years of long nights, missed birthdays, and sacrifices she'd never admitted out loud. She couldn't afford distractions now, not when she was so close.

She told herself she'd have to leave soon. Before things slipped any further. Before she started believing that slow mornings in a house that smelled like coffee and him could ever be hers.

It was time...had to be..to remember what mattered. *Her job. Her future.* Not this dangerous *almost* life.

Chapter Thirteen

Jackson

He leaned against the doorway, watching Molly as she curled up on his couch reading a book. The warm light softened her features, highlighting the curve of her cheek where she rested it against her hand. She appeared comfortable and at ease, but something else lingered. Something just beneath the surface.

She was pulling away.

Not obviously, but he could see it in the way she kept a little distance from him in the kitchen, and how she'd hesitated to talk about plans for next week. The thought of her leaving surfaced, but Jackson shoved it down. For now, she was still here. Tonight was theirs, and he intended to make the most of it.

He'd spent years returning to an empty house, and while it hadn't bothered him much before, the past few nights had changed him. Having someone to come home to, someone to cook for, someone waiting—it settled something deep inside him he hadn't realized was restless. Unable to resist, he stepped forward and leaned over the back of the couch. "Les Misérables? So, what do you think?"

She startled before stretching her arms in a slow, lazy motion. "He wasn't a bad guy. He just kept having bad things happen to him."

Jackson smirked, pleased she'd taken to the story. "Right. It's a chicken-and-egg situation." He reached out and tucked a stray curl behind her ear, enjoying the way her lips quirked up into something soft, something unguarded. "Ready to eat?"

Her smile widened. "Beyond ready. I'm starving."

"Good."

Jackson was more than ready to play host tonight. Hell, he'd been excited about this all day. He had everything planned out, every dish perfected with care. Ms. Sally had even given him a quick cooking lesson earlier that afternoon. She'd made sure he got her fried pickle recipe just right.

While growing up, his mom had shown him that cooking for someone was an act of love. If Molly was leaving soon, he could at least ensure she left with the memory of a comforting home-cooked meal. A meal that felt really important to him, even if he wasn't ready to admit why.

He carried each dish to the coffee table, laying out a spread meant to comfort and impress. Pasta salad filled a big bowl, along with a pot of chili, buttery corn on the cob, and—

"Fried pickles!"

Molly's excitement made his chest tighten with satisfaction. "I had some help," he said. "Ms. Sally gave me a lunchtime lesson and shared her secret family recipe. I had to swear to take it to my grave."

He barely had time to sit down before she grabbed a golden piece of fried batter, biting into it with an appreciative groan. "So good..." she said, reaching for another.

Jackson leaned back onto the couch, watching as she ate. It was strange how satisfying it was—watching her enjoy something he made, knowing he'd brought her a bit of comfort in a place that still likely felt unfamiliar.

"Don't forget the ranch." He nudged a small cup toward her. "You know, for the full experience."

She shot him a delighted look, and he thought, *"I could get used to this."*

After three fried pickle spears, she took a break. "What's next?"

Jackson smirked, handing her a steaming bowl. "My world-famous homemade chili. It's better after simmering all day, but that would've given away the surprise."

She took a cautious bite, only to fan at her lips. "Hot, hot—"

Jackson shook his head as he handed her a glass of milk. "Here's some milk. Your North is showing."

She shot him a glare before taking another bite. "It's got a kick, but there's something extra." She furrowed her brows in concentration before chewing. "It's tasty."

Jackson lifted his spoon. "Worcestershire sauce, honey, and celery," he admitted. "But don't tell my mom I told you."

"How'd you find time to take a cooking lesson, go shopping, handle the job site, and still come home this early?" she asked, watching him over the rim of her wineglass.

Jackson hesitated for only a fraction of a second before

answering. "I'll tell you later. I had to shift some things around."

He hesitated to mention the project delays and spoil the moment. She was already feeling disconnected, and he hated she wasn't on site to see the progress the Calypso was making. Duncan had things under control, but he knew it was eating at her.

Molly narrowed her eyes at his answer, but didn't press. "Is everything okay?"

"It will be." He gestured toward the plates still loaded with food. "Eat up."

She sighed in contentment, stretching against the couch. "You're a wonderful cook."

"I almost forgot!" Jackson said as he jumped up, then came back from the kitchen with two wine glasses and a bottle of Merlot. "I don't really know what I'm doing, but the wine guy said this would pair well with dinner. I figured it had to be better than the stuff in the box."

She lifted her glass of wine, took a slow sip, and hummed in approval. "That box stuff might surprise you, but this is better."

A grin tugged at the corner of his mouth as he leaned back in his seat. "You trust me now?"

She shook her head. "Never. But I'll give you this one."

They ate together, voices mingling with the hum of the house, and filling the space in a way that felt too natural. He tried not to think about it. He tried not to dwell on how effortlessly she fit into his life, into his routine. The way she curled up on his couch, stealing his books, leaving traces of herself in the simplest ways—her favorite cup in the kitchen, her boots near the door. It was easy to imagine what it would be like if she stayed.

Jackson never tried to make people stay after he'd learned the hard way that pushing too hard only drove them further away. He made that mistake with Jessica—loving her fiercely, but denying her the space she needed to grow. He'd held onto her, hoping their desires would align before she was ready.

He wouldn't make that mistake with Molly.

If she stayed, it needed to be because she wanted to. Not because he asked her to.

As he sank deeper into the couch, watching her rub her full stomach, he let himself imagine—just for a second—what it would be like if this were their routine. If she was there every night. If they built something together.

"How's it feeling?" he asked, breaking the silence.

She stretched, shifting to rest her feet in his lap, wincing as she moved. "Much better. A little sore, but I think I'll be back to normal soon."

He took her foot gently, pressing his thumbs in slow circles along the arch. "It's been nice having you here," he said, trying to sound casual even as his chest tightened.

She sighed, relaxing into his touch. "That feels amazing."

Jackson studied her, watching the way her shoulders eased, the way she finally seemed to let herself breathe. He wanted to give her more of that—quiet moments where she didn't have to be in charge of everything.

"You should let yourself pause sometimes," he said softly. "There's always another task, another distraction, but if you don't stop to breathe, you'll miss the best parts."

She huffed a quiet laugh. "So you're saying...remember to

breathe?"

His smile tilted. "Something like that."

The warmth in her eyes made his breath catch. Without thinking, his hand slid up, tracing the edge of her jeans where her pulse beat steady beneath his fingertips. His touch was light, careful, but it sent a spark through the quiet air between them.

She looked up at him, her expression shifting—open, curious. The moment hung suspended, weighted and fragile.

"Jackson..." Her voice was barely a whisper.

He swallowed, caught between want and restraint. "Yeah?"

"I'm curious," she murmured, eyes flicking to his mouth.

"About?"

"What this feels like," she said, the smallest smile ghosting across her lips.

He didn't answer with words. He leaned in slowly, giving her every chance to pull away. When she didn't, their lips met—soft, searching, and unhurried.

The world outside disappeared. The firelight flickered, painting them both in gold. Her fingers brushed his jaw; his hand came up to cradle the back of her neck. The kiss deepened, not rushed, but full of everything they hadn't said aloud.

When he pulled back, his voice was a low whisper. "Molly..."

She opened her eyes, dazed and smiling faintly. "Hmm?"

"Maybe...we should wait."

Her brow furrowed, but her smile stayed. "You're probably right."

He exhaled, the tension easing from his shoulders as he brushed his thumb along her cheek. "I just...don't want to mess this up."

"You won't," she said softly. "I trust you."

For a moment, neither of them spoke. The air between them was still charged, but it had shifted—less fire, more warmth.

Then she drew in a breath. "I think I should tell you what happened today."

He blinked, surprised by the change of tone, but nodded. "What happened?"

"I had to call off part of the crew."

Her spine straightened instantly. "And you didn't tell me earlier because...?"

He rubbed a hand over his face. "Because I knew you'd be upset, and I didn't want you to push yourself. I needed time to figure things out."

Her glare sharpened, all business again. "It's not your job to protect me from myself. You work for me on this project, Jackson."

He nodded once, steady. "Yes, ma'am."

He gathered their empty glasses and carried them to the kitchen. "Two issues came up today," he said over his shoulder. "First, we found black mold on the ground level. That means a quarantine and a specialized crew. It'll add another week, maybe two."

"Why can't the crew keep working on the upper floors?"

"Because they'd have to walk through the mold to get there."

"There has to be a way around it."

"Do you want me to use a crane to lift them up?"

"I'm going to guess that's a no."

"Pretty much."

"They won't be there anyhow," he continued. "With the delay, I'm moving most of the crew to another site until this is cleared."

Her arms crossed. "You what? You can't!"

"In truth, I can."

"We have a contract."

"One that I wrote, and you signed."

"How dare you—" The words burst out, then she winced. "I'm sorry. I thought we were past threatening contracts."

"I'm doing my job," he said, his tone clipped but calm.

Silence fell between them, heavy but not unkind.

Finally, she said quietly, "Maybe we should both sleep on it and talk tomorrow."

"You're probably right," he said, softening. "We'll know more after the specialists take a look."

When he stepped toward her, she held up a hand. "I think I can get upstairs myself tonight."

He nodded once.

At the top of the stairs, she paused and looked back. "Dinner was...nice. Goodnight."

He gave her a small smile. "Goodnight, Molly."

And because he'd learned the hard way what it meant to love and lose a strong woman—he let her go.

Chapter Fourteen

Molly

It was time for her to go. Molly could feel it. She was losing perspective—both in her work and in whatever this thing with Jackson had become.

When she woke that morning, she wasn't surprised to find him gone. He'd been leaving early all week, and she'd counted on it today.

What did surprise her was how hard it was to leave. She lingered—stalling over her half-packed bag, calling Ana to say she wouldn't need help after all, then assuring the skeptical secretary that everything was fine. The motions felt rehearsed, her voice sounding distant even to herself.

Leaving shouldn't have felt so difficult. She'd only been there a week. But somehow, she'd fallen into an easy rhythm with Jackson: coffee already made, quiet mornings, a sense of company that had slipped under her skin. She'd gotten comfortable in a fake housing scenario—playing house in a home that wasn't really hers.

So, she locked the front door behind her and went back to where she belonged.

The ride back to her hotel felt surreal.

In the short time she'd been with Jackson, Halloween had begun to creep into Texas—bright signs for haunted houses and costume shops flashing past the window. The world had kept moving while she'd been standing still. The heat still clung to the air, disguising the season, but the decorations told another story. Fall had arrived, and with it, a quiet reminder that she was running out of time.

In her hotel room, she unpacked the few things she'd had at Jackson's place. There wasn't much, just some simple house clothes, guest toiletries, and essentials he'd picked up. Fresh irritation simmered in her chest as she realized everything she'd had during the past couple of weeks had come from him.

The more she thought about it, the more it annoyed her. He'd controlled everything. She couldn't let herself believe it had been out of pure compassion or a simple desire to help her recover. Not that she'd been too exhausted to care, or too grateful for the momentary comfort he'd offered. No. Molly wasn't fragile. She didn't need anyone running her life for her.

To remind herself what was at stake, she grabbed her phone and called the office in Seattle. She exhaled a quiet sigh when Conner picked up. She missed Ana, too.

"NorthStar Properties, how can I help you?"

"Hi, Conner. It's Molly."

"Ms. Monroe! I wasn't expecting to hear from you. I figured you'd be at the Calypso, since Mr. Maherson and Paul are arriving today."

Her stomach dropped. "Excuse me—did you just say they arrive today?"

"Yes, didn't you get my message? I left it with the hotel."

"Ms. Monroe! I wasn't expecting to hear from you. I thought you'd be at the Calypso—Mr. Maherson and Paul are arriving today."

Her stomach dropped. *Arriving today.*

"What did you just say?"

"They're flying in this afternoon. Didn't you—"

But she'd already stopped listening. The realization hit hard: Conner had never called her cell. Whatever message he'd left at the hotel hadn't reached her, and now it didn't matter.

The explanation for his lapse in judgment was irrelevant—the damage was done.

"Of course," she said tightly. "Thank you, Conner." She ended the call before he could answer.

Fury burned white-hot. Jackson had gone over her head. And Paul, he was flying across the country without even telling her? Her pulse pounded as she shoved the anger down, forcing her voice into a smooth, overly sweet tone. "I...appreciate...the update, Conner. I'll need their itinerary emailed to me immediately. And when they get here, have them call me on my cell, not the hotel."

"I'll get right on it," Conner assured her.

She offered Conner a barely comprehensible, "Goodbye," before ending the call.

Before stepping through the gate onto the job site, Molly paused. She took a steadying breath, lifted her chin, and walked toward the hotel.

A group of men stood near the entrance. Even from a distance, she could pick out the tailored suits and soft build of two business executives—Paul and Mr. Maherson had already arrived. Standing slightly taller beside them, with a broader stance and a commanding presence, was Jackson Beaumont. He noticed her first.

She didn't think it was possible for him to look any bigger, but as soon as their eyes met, his shoulders pushed back, and the shift added another inch or two to his already formidable height. The tight clench of his jaw and the sharp pinch of his eyes told her exactly how he felt about seeing her that morning.

"Hello, gentlemen." Molly joined the group, doing her best to appear unfazed by the sight of her boss and co-worker standing outside a dirty hotel in Texas.

"Good morning, Molly. Glad you could join us." Paul's voice sounded anything but pleased, though Mr. Maherson didn't appear to notice.

"Molly! Glad you could make it. The Calypso is really shaping up. I was disappointed to hear about the mold, though."

"As was I, Mr. Maherson," she said, her voice smooth. "But Mr. Beaumont has a plan to keep us on schedule."

"Ms. Monroe." Jackson greeted her with a small nod, his

tone formal.

"I apologize for the delay. I was finishing up reviewing some reports." She gestured to her wrapped ankle. "It took me longer to get out of the hotel than I expected."

"Of course. Sorry to hear you were injured on our behalf, but you look well now. The Texas climate must agree with you." Mr. Maherson gave her an affable pat on the back before turning to Jackson. "Now that we're all here, let's discuss the revised plans."

Jackson hesitated for only a fraction of a second before addressing the assembled group. "We can iron out the final design decisions today. That way, we can order materials immediately and ensure prompt delivery. As long as the mold crew stays on schedule and we don't run into any other surprises, I expect we'll have the crew back in within a week to complete renovations for the December unveiling."

Paul barely seemed to listen. Instead, he narrowed his gaze at Molly. "Did you do something different with your hair?"

She exhaled slowly. "Trying to listen," she said, motioning toward Jackson.

Paul waved off her irritation. "Just making sure you're no t...losing focus out here."

Molly bristled. "Are you questioning my commitment to this job?"

Paul's gaze flickered down to her boots, then up over her jeans before settling on her face. "Not in the slightest," he said, as if the conversation had never happened. Then he turned back to Jackson, who finished outlining the interior adjustments.

"Molly and I have been discussing the budget limitations

and shipping constraints," Jackson said, his tone measured. "We believe this plan offers the best way forward."

Molly stood beside Paul, listening as Jackson kept his professionalism tight and controlled. His deep drawl could be thick as molasses or barely noticeable, and right now, he was definitely reining it in. It made her wonder why he had ever let her get close.

"Sounds fantastic, Jack." Mr. Maherson beamed before extending his hand for a firm shake. "As long as we stay on track, I trust you and Molly will keep everything moving smoothly."

"That's the plan."

As Paul and Mr. Maherson wandered the job site, nodding at progress and asking Duncan and the crew questions, Jackson stepped closer to her.

"What are you doing here?" His voice was hushed, but no less intense for it.

"My job."

"I made your excuses. They understood you couldn't be here today."

"That. Was. Not. Your. Place." Her words came out slow and deliberate.

Jackson exhaled sharply. "I don't understand why you couldn't sit out one meeting."

"This isn't about one meeting, Jackson. Do you know how hard it is to get those two out to a job site?" She motioned toward Paul and Mr. Maherson, who were carefully sidestepping puddles and avoiding bustling contractors. "Something has to go wrong first."

"They don't seem panicked."

"They're sharks. You won't know you're dead until you're bleeding out." Her expression hardened. "You gave them blood, Jackson. I can't afford to show weakness right now. If I want this promotion, I need to be here."

His frown deepened. "Have you thought about letting the promotion go?"

Her frustration clogged her throat, hot and suffocating. Without another word, she pivoted on her heel and walked away before she did something reckless—like punch him square in the jaw.

She'd had no trouble convincing Paul and Mr. Maherson to move their discussion to a cooler, more refined setting. They spent the afternoon catching up over bourbon and linen napkins. The local steak house, A Rare Affair, was the perfect place to fuel their enthusiasm, curating a vision for what the hotel was becoming.

They discussed the opening gala—a sophisticated gathering of local influencers, celebrating the restoration and welcoming the project into Serenity's tightly knit business community. On top of renovating and outfitting an extravagant hotel, their first night open would host Serenity's wealthiest and most influential citizens. When she finally said goodbye to her boss and coworker, her head buzzed with a never-ending list of things to plan.

For the briefest moment, she considered flying Conner down to help, but the idea of spending the next eight weeks working at his side made her jaw clench.

As soon as she stepped into her hotel room, she peeled off her work clothes, trading them for the comforting embrace of old, soft pajamas. "No more distractions," she told herself—just as she noticed the blinking light on the room phone.

"No..." She exhaled. "If Conner screwed up again—" Bracing herself for the worst, she picked up the phone and hit play.

"Where are you?" Jackson's voice was rough, clipped, and then the message ended.

She debated calling him back, but she simply couldn't afford this complication right now.

Instead, she texted Ana, *What are you doing?*

I'll call, give me 5

When her phone rang, she barely let it complete the first buzz before answering.

"You didn't have to call," she said.

"Oh, yes, I did." Ana's voice brimmed with mischief. "What did you do to Jackson?"

"I didn't do a thing! He just...didn't want me to leave."

Ana was silent on the other end, but Molly could hear Marco talking in the background.

"I know! I know, I'm on the phone!" Ana muttered, apparently to him.

"Do I need to—?"

"With Molly!"

"I can—"

"No, she didn't break Jackson." Ana sighed dramatically. "Really!"

Molly raised an eyebrow. "Ana?"

"Yeah, yeah, I'm leaving the room." A door clicked in the background, and Ana's voice lowered. "So, you left without telling him?"

Molly flopped onto her bed. "I'm a coward. I didn't want to have that conversation."

"You hurt his feelings."

"If it's any consolation, I hurt my feelings, too." Her throat tightened, and she pressed a hand to her face.

Ana paused before relenting. "A little, I guess." Then, after a pause, she asked, "So what's got you calling this late?"

"Want a job?"

Ana's laugh was immediate. "Ha! He'd kill us both."

"It's temporary—weekends, evenings. I need help keeping this project under control *and* planning the unveiling event."

Ana hesitated. "Can I think about it? Call you tomorrow?"

"Sure. I'll let you get back to Marco. He sounds like he's about to explode."

"Well, he's a big Jackson fan, and doesn't want me taking sides."

"You know I'd never ask that," Molly reassured her. "We just...won't tell him you're helping me."

"*Maybe* helping you."

Molly grinned. "I'll email you the details. Then you can decide."

"Deal."

After they hung up, Molly looked around her hotel room. Though it hadn't been long, staying at Jackson's made the hotel feel all wrong. The sleek furnishings and cool tones felt more corporate than cozy. A thought crept in.

Serenity wasn't like other places. The Calypso needed to feel different—like an experience, not just a hotel stay.

There was a minimalist square desk in the corner next to a modern high-backed chair covered in a dark gray brushed velvet. A matching love seat and a dresser with a built-in mini fridge completed the room. Despite having all the amenities she needed, it still felt like the bed sat in the middle of an office suite.

What would set their hotel apart from all the others? They needed it to be unique. Like an individualized piece of art...that vein of creativity could be their focus.

Modern design mixed with something *real*. Minimalist couches strewn with flamboyant throw pillows individualized by local artists, rooms that featured high end espresso machines and top of the line toiletries. Light fixtures that invoked awe when they lit up a room with tendrils, or spirals, or in kaleidoscopes of color.

She grabbed a notebook and started writing. She wrote until her eyes burned and exhaustion weighed her down.

A small tinge of anxiety pinched her gut when she realized she'd have to call Jackson in the morning to talk about the potential changes.

One thing at a time.

She kept scribbling until sleep finally claimed her—without even climbing under the blankets on the bed.

Chapter Fifteen

Molly

"Were you trying to make a point?" Jackson didn't even bother with a hello. His voice poured through the phone, deep and edged with frustration. "Because if you were, I get it. I'm sorry I interfered with your job."

Molly sank deeper into the chair in her hotel room, her fingers tightening around the phone. She closed her eyes and exhaled through her nose, willing her muscles to loosen. "I wasn't making a point, Jackson. At least not intentionally." She traced small circles against her temple with her free hand, pressing against the dull ache settling in. "These are my responsibilities. I'm just getting back to them."

A long pause.

Then, quieter, roughened by something unreadable, "I missed you last night."

The grip on her phone faltered slightly.

She squeezed her eyes shut, bracing herself, trying to ignore the way his words unsettled something deep inside her, something she wasn't ready to name.

"You'll get used to it," she said, forcing her voice to sound cool and detached.

The noises on the other end of the line surged—a muffled clang of metal, the grind of machinery, voices calling out over the sound of labor. Barely above the noise, Jackson's voice came through, again, softer this time. "What if I don't want to?"

Molly's fingers curled over the hotel comforter, pressing into the fabric. "Where are you?"

"At a job site."

A tension, slow and creeping, curled into her shoulders. "The one that replaced mine?"

Silence stretched for just a second too long.

"I haven't replaced you," Jackson said. "There was a delay."

The tension shifted, gripping at the base of her neck. She leaned forward, bracing her elbow against her knee. "I'd like to talk about some design changes." The words came out stiff, professional. It was one thing she could control. "This delay might actually help me."

Something shifted in his tone, curiosity peeking through the exasperation. "Interesting." A pause. "We can discuss them over dinner. My place?"

Molly let out a short, humorless laugh. "Nice try. No."

"Ms. Sally's been asking about you."

Her stomach unexpectedly flipped, warmth flickering beneath her simmering frustration. "I think we should meet somewhere professional," she said, shaking off the thought. "I don't want us to get," her voice wavered, betraying her, "distracted."

The line went quiet for half a breath, and then, smooth as whiskey, he said, "Too late."

A sound of hammering, shouting, boots crunching against concrete. Everything else was gone, buried by the weight behind his words.

Molly pressed a fingertip to her temple, swallowing down the heat creeping up her throat. "Just send me the details," she said, ignoring the unspoken challenge between them.

"Sure," Jackson answered, with a smirk. "And I'll bring Ana—she can take notes."

Her shoulders softened slightly. A minor concession. A line drawn. "I appreciate you keeping this professional," she said, though the words felt foreign.

"That makes one of us," he said under his breath before clearing his throat. "Gotta go."

"All right," Molly said, pushing up from her chair, pacing as she processed the conversation. "Talk later. Bye."

She hung up. A frown tugged at the corners of her lips as she immediately dialed Paul in Seattle. Her mind was already shifting away from maybes and wishes, towards strategies and progress.

He answered on the second ring, his tone light. "Howdy, partner."

"Ha, ha, very funny." Molly sighed. "Seriously though, I think I've stumbled on a great idea for the Calypso remodel."

She outlined her vision with precision. Every detail sharp in her mind: the clean sophistication of New York's polished art scene, the stylistic soul of Seattle's creative hubs, the welcoming touch of Texas hospitality. A hotel that wasn't just a destination, but an experience.

Molly described walking guests into a place that breathed inspiration. Walls that showcased striking pieces from local painters, sculptors, textile artists. Furniture that wasn't just bought, but made with rich, reclaimed wood, handcrafted linens infused with quiet histories, lighting not merely for brightness, but for spectacle. A lobby bathed in contrast. There would be sleek monochromes against bursts of brilliance, reflecting the way Serenity balanced old Texas charm with community and innovation.

When she finally finished, she exhaled, waiting for his response. The silence stretched a little too long.

Then, finally, Paul sighed. "Molly, that's old news. You can't get those kinds of changes done in the time we have left. Plus, Mr. Maherson's focus is on a more contemporary design."

She shook her head, gripping the phone tighter. "Paul, this *is* contemporary. It's unique, and we have nothing else like this in our portfolio. There is *nothing* like this in Texas. People will line up to stay here. You have my word."

Another sigh. "I'll talk to Mr. Maherson and get back to you."

"That's all I ask." The tension at the base of her skull eased, just slightly. "Thanks, Paul."

When she hung up, she pressed her hand to her forehead, inhaling slowly. The plan was solid. She knew it was.

Now, she had two negotiations to win.

One with Paul.

And one with Jackson.

Because no matter how many headaches he caused her, she

needed him to be on board. She needed him to *see* what she saw. And, if she was being honest with herself, maybe...just maybe...she needed him to see *her*, too.

By the end of the day, Molly had meticulously outlined every detail of the unveiling down to the curated menu, the entertainment lineup, and the precise timing of presentations. Immersed in her work, she lost track of time until her phone buzzed, pulling her from her well-ordered plans.

"You ready?" Ana's voice was warm. "I was thinking I'd come get you."

Molly blinked, glancing at the mess of papers scattered across her hotel room. Charts, fabric swatches, expense reports—her temporary office had turned into controlled chaos. "That sounds nice," she said, already thinking about what she could feasibly clean up before heading out.

"Perfect! I'm already downstairs. Hurry."

"Oh." Molly exhaled sharply. "Bossy, aren't you?"

"You love it."

Hanging up, she spun around, surveying the disaster zone she'd created. A small mountain of sketch pads and vendor quotes buried the dresser. Her suitcase, abandoned next to the bed, had become a secondary desk, its contents half-unpacked, blending with the mess.

From the piles, she unearthed a vibrant red cotton skirt Taylor had convinced her to buy. She nearly tripped over a stack of folded blueprints while stepping into the embroidered waistband. She swore softly, hopping on one foot as she yanked the skirt into place. Near the door were her boots, broken in just enough to be comfortable.

Pausing at the mirror, she studied herself. Recent months had left a faint weariness in the curve of her mouth, but there was a brightness in her expression tonight. The warm glow of the hotel light highlighted her hair, the unruly curls growing fuller in the humid air. She finger-combed the strands, debating whether to tame them. Instead, she tilted her head, letting the golden waves fall wildly. The dusty boots and cotton skirt empowered her with a combination of grit and femininity. "Work hard, play hard."

She almost laughed at herself. Two months ago, she had painstakingly straightened every piece before stepping into a boardroom. Now, the Texas heat was bringing out some part of her she hadn't realized she had been repressing. Satisfied, she grabbed her purse and hurried for the door.

Outside, Ana's Honda Pilot idled by the curb, its headlights casting long streaks of light across the pavement. "You're late." Ana barely glanced up from her phone as Molly buckled in.

"You're dramatic! I didn't even know you were coming."

Ana smirked before tossing her phone into her bag and pulling onto the street. "Where we're going, late is unacceptable."

Molly raised a brow. "Should I be worried?"

Ana's grin widened. "Not yet."

The car navigated the evening streets, weaving through downtown. Houston was alive at night, the skyline glittering against the dark expanse of sky. Brake lights flared red in the dense holiday traffic, and Molly watched as drivers impatiently switched lanes, their movements sharp with frustration. Here, far from Seattle's rain-slicked streets, the pulse of the city was different—more sprawling, less hurried.

Molly's fingers drummed against her knee. "Where are we going?"

"It's a surprise."

"This is supposed to be a business meeting."

Ana snorted. "Yeah, well, we think differently about business than you do."

Molly turned her head, studying her. "'We?'"

"How do you feel about line dancing?"

Molly blinked. "I don't think I have any feelings about it." A brief pause. "Though I suspect I will by the end of tonight."

Ana laughed. "Well, we take it seriously."

Molly exhaled, shaking her head.

They fought through the thick congestion of the freeway, the car weaving through the maze of headlights. The mix of honking, rumbling engines, and faintly audible music from nearby cars created a symphony of movement. Ana navigated the streets with casual expertise, her fingers tapping the steering wheel to an unheard rhythm.

"Thanks for driving." Molly stretched her legs. "I have the rental, but the thought of fighting Houston traffic and parking downtown after today is soul-crushing."

"Are you kidding? If you drove, how would I get all the company gossip?"

"What gossip?" Molly asked with a scoff.

Ana shot her a sidelong glance, expression knowing. "Don't

play innocent. I've seen how he watches you. Besides, you two can't keep your hands off each other."

Molly's immediate protest died faster than her dignity. "They're back pats and hello hugs."

Ana rolled her eyes, long and slow.

"Fine," Molly said, running a hand through her hair. "We can't be alone together. I'm struggling to keep things professional."

Ana grinned, triumphant.

"You and I got drunk in the office the first day we met," she pointed out. "Let's not pretend professional was the goal."

"I know, but this opportunity is massive for my career. I can't screw it up."

"Life isn't all about your career, Molly."

"Some of us don't have a Marco," Molly countered. "This is what I've always wanted. It's the reward for all my sacrifice and hard work."

Ana was quiet for a moment before saying, softer than before, "Did it ever occur to you that you don't have a Marco because of your job?"

The words struck harder than Molly wanted to admit. She rested her elbow against the window, her fingers brushing her lower lip thoughtfully.

"Whose side are you on?" she asked, though there was an edge buried beneath the question.

"I'm not taking sides," Ana said. "I want to make sure you're happy. If this is what you want, I support you 100%." She tapped a hand against the center console, considering. "In fact, I talked to Marco. He says I can help you on evenings and weekends—as long as it doesn't hurt Jackson."

Molly's head turned sharply. "How would it hurt him? His name's on this, too. He'll probably get jobs for years because of it."

Ana shot her a look, leveling her with a single raised eyebrow—clearly asking, *Do you think I'm that dumb?* Then she turned back to the road and continued driving.

Molly understood the silent accusation immediately.

She exhaled, turning her eyes back to the blur of city lights streaking past the window.

Ana didn't press further. She didn't need to.

Molly already knew.

Jackson wasn't the one who would get hurt.

She was.

Chapter Sixteen

Molly

When they finally pulled up outside a dilapidated old wooden building, Molly peered out and asked, "Really? The Old Wagon Wheel?"

Molly climbed out of the car with Ana and glanced around. The palm trees lining the street looked out of place next to the faded wood paneled front of the old dance hall, bar, and restaurant. The thumping country music inside was audible even from the parking lot. A Garth Brooks classic.

She knew enough about country music to recognize a fan favorite when she heard one. As the lyrics to "Friends in Low Places" drifted out, and Ana started singing along.

When she pushed open the front door, the music poured over them, wrapping them in the familiar melody. Molly hesitated for a moment before following Ana inside.

Every table was full, the dance floor was ringed with standing patrons, and the bar buzzed with conversation. From across the room, she spotted Jackson seated towards the back. He raised a hand in greeting, and they made their way toward him. Molly bumped into a few people, but no one seemed to mind.

"So much for a work meeting," she said once they reached him.

"We'll get plenty of work done," Jackson assured her with a smirk. "But first, we're going to show you more of what makes Texas special."

As the song ended and a new one started, Jackson stood and extended his hand. The first notes of a honky tonk ballad played over the speakers, and an announcer took the stage to guide the crowd through a series of dance steps.

"Come on. It's not that hard," he said.

Molly hesitated, "I want to careful for my foot—"

"Okay," Jackson pulled her close. "I'll treat you gently."

Ana nudged them towards the dance floor.

They walked through the choreography once before the music restarted. Jackson was impossible to keep up with. Every step was crisp, and every movement effortless. His smile was electric, lighting up his entire face. Earlier, he'd patiently helped her through the steps, but now he was completely in tune with the music.

She was relieved to find she wasn't completely terrible. Her years as a cheerleader had ingrained the fundamentals of counting beats and memorizing sequences. After a few songs, she was getting the hang of it, and started enjoying herself. She laughed as she moved in sync with the crowd.

Jackson's approving glances and steady touches guiding her through the routine sent a thrill through her. She hadn't expected line dancing to feel both distant and intimate. The structured movements kept them apart, but in fleeting moments, they came close enough that she felt the warmth of his body.

Each time their hands brushed, or he guided her with a light touch, her heart pounded a little harder. Twice, she nearly lost track of the steps, too distracted by how effortless it would be to fall completely into his arms. After a few rounds, she returned to the table, grinning ear to ear.

Ana smirked. "Still mad?"

Molly gave him the side-eye. "You know the answer to that." She grew serious. "I still want to talk about the Calypso."

"We will."

Molly barely had time to catch her breath before she felt a tap on her shoulder. Turning, she looked up at a tall, blonde cowboy in a white Stetson and a snug pair of well-worn jeans.

"May I have this dance?"

Without a reason to refuse, she smiled and accepted. From the dance floor, she caught Jackson watching her. His expression darkened as he downed the beer in his hand before immediately ordering another.

By the time she returned to the table, Jackson was glaring at both her and her dance partner.

"Nice moves," he said, raising his glass in a mock toast to them.

The blond cowboy met his gaze for a moment before dipping his head slightly. "Pleasure dancing with you, ma'am." With another polite tip of his hat, he turned and sauntered away.

Molly crossed her arms. "Seriously, Jackson? Why don't you just piss on me and be done with it?"

"That wouldn't be very gentlemanly."

"Well, neither is the way you're acting."

"He's not a terrible dancer," Jackson allowed, nodding toward the retreating cowboy.

"He was an excellent teacher too—almost as good as you." She leaned back in her chair, still breathless from the dancing. "I think I'm getting the hang of this. Though perhaps it's time to slow down," she said, wiggling her ankle in her boot.

Jackson smirked, but chose not to argue. He shifted the conversation and asked, "So, this big idea for the Calypso?"

Her frustration vanished in an instant. She practically vibrated with excitement. "I want to create a hotel that's more than a place to stay—it should be an experience. A museum, a retreat, something that feeds the soul as much as the body. Imagine home-cooked cuisine, breathtaking art, and a design that makes the Calypso stand out from anything else."

"I'm listening. How do you plan to pull this off?"

"We need to rework some of the original plans. I want to make this a community-driven project. We should as much as possible from local suppliers. Our design will be environmentally mindful and unique. I envision a LED light wall that interacts with guests as they arrive. A lobby with hammocks. Staying at the Calypso should be fun and inspiring."

Jackson rested his chin on his hand, considering her words. "What does Maherson say about all this?"

"Paul told me he'd bring it up today. I'm hoping the vision will resonate. It's risky, sure—but being different is what will make it special. I want the Calypso to be as exciting for visitors as Disneyland is for kids."

"And what do you need from me?"

Molly met his gaze. "I need you to be open to change. Be flexible. The existing design has wonderful elements—the minimalist furniture, the chrome finishes—we're halfway there. But we need to shift the color scheme. We can make slight changes in design and sourcing that will have a big impact. No more browns and heavy earth tones. I want the Calypso to be a canvas for art. Black, white—anything that contrasts with vibrant displays. The goal is to engage hearts and minds the moment people step inside." She licked her lips. "I need you to help me bring this vision to life."

Jackson reached across the table, brushing his fingers lightly against hers. "Can we talk somewhere private?"

She hesitated. "I don't know if that's a good idea."

"I want five minutes." His eyes warmed, making it impossible to refuse. "I want to talk about what happened."

With a sigh, she nodded. He led her to a door behind the stage, opening it to reveal a back patio. The humid night enveloped them. That same smell she associated with Texas hung in the air.

The patio was lit with small fairy lights that hung in the palm tree. Their fronds created a canopy of privacy. "Why did you leave?"

"I couldn't stay."

"Why not?"

"Because we're working together, Jackson. If anyone found out—"

"They might understand."

"No, they wouldn't. We're talking millions of dollars. If this project fails, I'll be the one they blame for being distracted."

He stepped closer, his hand lifting to trace a whisper-soft path down the side of her neck, pausing at her shoulder before continuing its slow descent down her arm. When his fingers threaded through hers, she felt a spark ignite within her. "I didn't want you to leave that way, Molly." His voice was raw, barely more than a whisper. "I didn't want you to leave at all."

He took another step towards her, closing the gap between them until they were mere inches apart. She could feel his breath on her face, see the intensity in his eyes. "I didn't want to leave like that either," she admitted, her voice soft. "But I didn't see another way."

Her free hand found its way to his side, her thumb tracing the edge of his shirt. She felt his breath catch under her touch.

"This," she whispered, her voice barely audible. "We're sneaking around in the dark instead of focusing on the work."

"We talked business," he countered softly, a hint of laughter in his voice. Taking her hand, he pressed a gentle kiss to her fingertips before turning it over to brush his thumb across her palm. The simple contact sent a flutter through her chest. "There's room for a little pleasure, too."

She let out a quiet sound of agreement, the corners of her mouth lifting. The space between them seemed to disappear without either of them moving. He lifted her chin with his free hand, and their eyes met just before his lips found hers in a slow, tender kiss.

The world fell away. The sounds of the city softened, replaced by the steady rhythm of two hearts finding the same beat.

His arms came around her, holding her close, steady and sure. She felt the warmth of his body, the strength of him, and how completely safe she felt in his embrace. Her breath trembled against his cheek, a soft sigh that carried everything she couldn't say out loud.

When he shifted, guiding her gently back against the wall, she didn't resist. The night air was cool, but his nearness chased away the chill. He brushed a kiss against her temple, a wordless promise more tender than urgent.

For a moment, she closed her eyes, memorizing the feel of being held like that—protected, seen, understood.

Every sense was awake, but it wasn't just attraction; it was recognition, the kind that made staying away from him feel impossible.

Chapter Seventeen

Jackson

The need to be close to her was overwhelming. It was a pull Jackson couldn't ignore. When she braced herself against his shoulders, swaying with him to the soft beat of the music drifting through the courtyard, every inch of him came alive.

Her arms slipped around his neck, fingers tangling in his hair as she kissed him, deepening it with a tenderness that made his pulse stutter. Every nerve in his body sparked to life.

He groaned softly against her mouth, hands finding her waist, feeling the steady rise and fall of her breath beneath his palms. She fit against him as though they'd been made to move together, their rhythm falling into sync with the faint music and the far-off murmur of laughter inside.

"Jackson," she whispered, her voice a plea and a promise all at once.

He pressed his forehead to hers, breathing her in—the faint scent of citrus and warmth and something that would undo him if he let it. "You have no idea what you're doing to me," he murmured.

Her quiet laugh trembled against his lips. "Maybe I do."

He chuckled low, brushing his thumb along her jaw before leaning in again. Their kiss slowed, deepened—less about hunger now, more about the simple, dizzying joy of being known and wanted.

The world beyond the courtyard disappeared. The lights from the party glowed through the glass doors, a reminder of how close they were to being seen, but neither of them pulled away. It wasn't about recklessness anymore. It was about a heartbeat shared between two people who'd been dancing around this moment for far too long.

Then, with a sudden bang, the patio door flew open.

Jackson froze, instincts kicking in as a drunk couple stumbled onto the deck, laughing and pawing at each other. He jerked back, sliding an arm in front of Molly, instinctively shielding her from view.

Heart pounding, he kept his body angled toward the newcomers, waiting—until they veered left, giggling and weaving toward a dark corner of the patio.

Molly exhaled shakily. Jackson turned back to her, brushing a loose strand of hair from her face, his smile small and full of everything he couldn't yet say.

"Guess the universe wanted to keep us honest," he murmured.

She laughed softly, still breathless. "Maybe for tonight."

Molly wiggled slightly behind him, straightening her clothes. Jackson didn't turn around. He wouldn't take even a second of her privacy.

Already, regret tightened his chest—not because he didn't want her. God, he wanted her. But because he'd promised himself he wouldn't push. Not with her. Not now.

He finally risked a glance over his shoulder. She was still catching her breath, cheeks flushed, hair a little mussed, her lips soft and swollen from their stolen kisses. She met his gaze, and for a long, aching moment, neither of them spoke.

A different version of him might've made a joke, or tried to laugh it off. But right now, his pulse thudded hard in his chest, raw with the weight of how close he'd come to crossing a line he didn't want to blur.

He reached back, offering her his hand. "I think that's a sign." She hesitated for a moment, then squeezed his hand. His heart thudded, the small connection grounding him. "Ana will be waiting."

They slipped back inside together, the shift in atmosphere almost jarring. Country music thudded through the floor, familiar and grounding, but everything felt a little more intense now—tighter in his skin. Her heat still lingered on his chest, her curves still molded into his memory, and the taste of her was burned into his mouth.

They returned to the table where Ana was waiting. "What happened to you two?" she asked, brow raised.

Jackson met Molly's eyes for half a second. He could feel his ears heating, but he didn't let it show. Molly recovered first.

"I wasn't feeling well. We stepped outside for some fresh air," she offered calmly.

Ana paused, clearly not buying the excuse, but she nodded. "You could've told me. Are you okay? Do we need to go home?"

Jackson reached into his pocket, pulling out his keys with a flick of his wrist. "I'll take her back to the Calypso. No sense in you being out late with Marco waiting at home." He wanted to get Molly away from this place. The moment outside had taken them both somewhere a little too dangerous.

Ana gave Molly a look, silent but sharp. "You sure?"

Molly nodded. "Yeah. Thanks for tonight. My feet will hate me tomorrow, but it was worth it."

Jackson slid his keys into his palm, knuckles brushing against her as they turned for the door. They were only three steps from the table where Ana still sat when he felt it. There was a quiet ache crawling up his spine.

As they left, he saw couples holding hands, leaning into each other during slow songs, and spinning gently across the wood floor. He watched them, and for the first time in a long time, something unfamiliar settled into the back of his throat.

Jealousy.

He wanted that.

He wanted her.

Not just for a kiss, not just for entertainment, or a night together. He wanted the nights that came afterwards. The soft kind, with her curled beside him in his bed, her laughter in his kitchen, the way she'd quietly lean her head on his shoulder without saying a thing.

Street lamps and headlights from passing cars lit up the truck cab. God, she'd looked beautiful under the neon lights.

"Thanks for the ride,"

He nodded. "Any time." He reached for her hand without thinking, but pulled back before his fingers could touch hers. "Did you have fun tonight?"

"Yeah, I did."

"You're quiet."

"I'm thinking."

His jaw worked shut for a second as he glanced down at her. "About what?"

Her answer hit low and sudden. "What happened on that patio?"

"Yeah," he said, voice dropped deep and raw, "I was thinking about that, too."

Her hair curled around her neck. Her pulse was visible just beneath her collarbone. He couldn't resist glancing down to her thick thighs and where her skirt stretched over her hips—the same hips he'd crushed into the wall not thirty minutes ago. She'd situated herself, eyes forward, but he could tell she was just as turned on as he was.

Every inch of him still buzzed. He slid behind the wheel, rolling the windows down to breathe cooler air.

"I like how you always have me out in the fresh air under the stars," she said.

"I like how you light up at night."

She laughed gently, turning her head toward him. "That sounds suspiciously like a line."

He forced himself to smirk, but his gut was tight. "And if it is?"

Her eyes met his, softened though electric. "Then I'd say..

.it's working."

He sucked in a breath. "Good," he said, then paused. "I want more than stolen moments. I'm not okay with 'some time' before you leave."

It cost him something to say it out loud. It hurt saying those words, watching her, and knowing that if nothing changed, she wouldn't be his past Christmas.

"Neither am I,"

For a second, the air pulsed with things better left unsaid. Fifty different thoughts pulsed through him...tell her to stay, tell her you'd give everything for a shot, or tell her lips you don't want to taste anyone else.

She bumped his shoulder affectionately, diffusing the tension, which allowed him to breathe.

"But you still have work to do...especially on your sweet talk."

"I'm not sure I can improve on that last one," he said, hands tightening around the wheel. "But, if you keep letting me steal you away," he added, quieter now. "I'll take my chances."

Chapter Eighteen

Molly

"That's amazing, Paul!"

"Yes, really. Your ideas excited Maherson. He called them groundbreaking and said he's eager to see where this takes us." Paul hesitated, his voice softening. "Off the record—he nearly handed you the promotion on the spot. He just wants to see the unveiling in December go smoothly."

"I'll make sure it does," Molly said, her pulse racing.

"I know you will," Paul replied warmly. "You've earned this."

When the call ended, she exhaled, giddy. She threw on her work pants, grabbed her keys, and checked her watch—noon. "He said one," she murmured. Nothing could ruin this day.

Jackson had promised good news, and from what she'd heard, the mold removal had gone smoothly. With the recent changes nearly in place and her confidence high, she had time to spare—and the Texas sun was shining.

On a whim, she detoured to Patty Cakes and picked up an

assortment of donuts and kolaches to surprise the crew.

She'd quickly fallen in love with the soft, yeasty bread stuffed with spicy meat and cheese. Texas had a lot going for it, but the food easily topped the list. The warm box rested on the passenger seat as she navigated traffic toward the job site.

When she arrived and saw Jackson's truck missing, her gut tightened. The kolache in her mouth turned to tasteless dough. Jackson not being on site was never a good sign. Duncan, already directing a delivery truck, waved at her as she climbed out of the car.

"Where's Jackson?" she asked immediately.

"Got pulled somewhere else," Duncan said, shifting uncomfortably.

Molly didn't waste time pressing him. She called Jackson.

It surprised her when he picked up on the second ring. "Everything okay?"

"No," she said tightly. "Why aren't you on-site?"

"A delay came up—Ana's handling this."

"I need you here, Jackson."

"I can't. Another job's taking priority."

She froze. "Since when?"

"A few days ago. Look, why don't you come here? I'll explain."

She jotted down the address he gave her and plugged it into her GPS app. The map recalculated twice before settling. She frowned at the screen. "Are you sure about this address?"

He glanced at it, hesitated, and asked, "Yeah, are you sure?"

"Yes." Molly was ready to see what had been distracting Jackson from her job.

The farther they drove, the more she understood Duncan's concern. Downtown streets gave way to cracked sidewalks, boarded-up windows, and fading painted walls layered with graffiti. Parked alongside expensive Escalades and BMWs were old Hondas and Kias—cars that hadn't come from a typical nine-to-five day job.

She pulled up outside the old brick building and sat there for a beat, engine idling. Her instincts flared—the kind that usually told her to stay in the car.

Jackson's truck sat parked on the street nearby.

"Molly, you're good," she murmured to herself.

The neighborhood was quiet. Empty streets stretched ahead, but not the kind abandoned out of fear. Flowers bloomed stubbornly in crumbling planters, sun-bleached clothes swayed on sagging lines, and hints of poverty clung to everything.

Jackson met her in the parking lot of a dilapidated cinder block building. "Glad you came."

"I'm not sure why you asked me here." She looked around at the aging playground nearby and the faded handwritten signs tapped on the old building. "What is this place?"

"Come on," he said, taking her hand. "I want to show you something. It's overdue."

As he led her inside, she caught glimpses of faded children's artwork on the walls, and a worn-out receptionist's desk stood at the entrance.

"Where are we?" she asked again.

"A community center," he said. "Or what's left of one..."

The fluorescent lighting cast bleak shadows, but kids ran through the halls with bright smiles. Signs advertised ballet, Tae Kwon Do, sewing, cooking, and classes for everyone in the family.

Molly's chest tightened. "Are you working here?"

Jackson sighed. "A fire took out the gym and kitchen. They barely had enough funding to operate before this. Now, no one else wants to do the repairs without upfront payment."

She could see what he wasn't saying.

"You *chose* this over the Calypso," she said.

"I *had* to." His voice was firm. "I grew up coming here, Molly. The families keeping this place alive— they have nowhere else to go. The kids need a safe space. Parents need after-school care. If no one stepped in..." He shook his head. "I know the Calypso is important to you, but *this* is important to me. I'm still doing everything I promised you. We have a good crew, and I trust them. So, I am doing *both*."

Molly glanced around at the children, the mothers chatting further down the hallway, and the small group of kids leaving a craft class. Life thrived here, while the Calypso gave solely to its investors.

She *wanted* anger. Then she could tell Jackson his commitment *should* have been to their contract. Instead, she asked, "Why didn't you tell me sooner?"

His lips pressed into a thin line. "I didn't want you thinking I was manipulating you." He hesitated. "And maybe you left before I had the chance."

Molly ignored that last part. "So, what's the plan? What are you going to do?"

"Duncan's managed every job I've ever done. Ana keeps materials moving. As long as everything stays on track, we'll finish the Calypso on schedule."

"You believe that?" she asked.

"It's the best I've got."

A boy sprinted past them, a girl with black hair hot on his heels. A second later, two mothers followed, pushing strollers and laughing.

Molly saw it clearly now. This wasn't only Jackson's responsibility. It belonged to everyone in this town.

"I'm taking over," she said.

Jackson blinked. "What?"

"You're the contractor. I'll manage getting people's attention. This is my job now."

"Molly—"

"This is the responsibility of everyone in this community. Each one of the store owners, residents, or civil service workers. Everyone in this town owes something to this building. I'm sure every upstanding citizen, educated child, and loving community member has had a chance to attend, teach or watch a class, concert, or event here. This place matters. And I'm going to make sure everyone remembers that."

Jackson studied her, then asked, "And how do you plan to do that?"

Molly lifted her chin. "Just you wait."

Chapter Nineteen

Molly

Having a microphone shoved in her face was awkward, but the redheaded reporter behind it smiled warmly, making the experience easier to bear.

"So, Ms. Monroe, please tell us what brings you here today."

Molly glanced around, watching as the film crew interviewed the mothers, children, and neighbors that had gathered to support the community center. "We're here to rescue this building. It's been a cornerstone of the community for years. This building has seen a lot of love, and recently suffered from some pretty costly repairs. The center's management simply can't afford to fix the critical items. I was hoping you would help us spread the word. We need help."

"This place is incredible," the reporter said. "Tell us more about how the center helps the community."

"Well, I know Grover Sheen, from down at the Mercantile, learned to two-step with his wife here before their wedding. Ms.

Imogene learned to sew here. Her very first real project was a christening dress for her new grand baby. Just last month, the Nielsen twins had their first ballet recital in the gymnasium."

"What will happen to this center if the repairs don't happen?"

Molly turned, reaching for Jackson, who stood behind her speaking with a concerned parent. Pulling him into the camera frame, she said, "This is Jackson Beaumont. He's the contractor working to fix things up, but he needs help. He won't be able to finish all the repairs on his own. To put it simply, this place will close."

For a moment, Jackson froze, his eyes widening in a classic deer-in-the-headlights expression. His body tensed beside hers.

Then the reporter smiled. "Oh, sir, you're amazing. Every community needs a hero like you."

Molly felt the tension drain from Jackson's body as a slow smile spread across his face. Apparently, ego-stroking goes a long way.

"Well, ma'am, it's really nothing," he said, rubbing the back of his neck. "I wish I could do more, but it's a busy time of year, and I don't have enough hands to get it all done."

He spoke for a few more minutes before the reporter wrapped up the interview. "Thank you, Mr. Beaumont. These kinds of stories are exactly what the people love to hear."

Jackson shook his head. "This was never about me. I hope the broadcast inspires people to step up and help out. The holidays are coming up, and it's the perfect time to give back."

⚙

"I don't know how you pulled that off," Jackson admitted, watching as workers hustled around the site.

It wasn't long before donations and volunteers had poured in. Local electricians, plumbers, and carpenters arrived, eager to help. Businesses sent supplies, food, clothing, and household goods. By the week's end, they had enough money and materials to complete the remodel.

Molly smirked. "A wise bird once told me you catch more bees with honey than vinegar. First, I appealed to their hearts."

"A handsome contractor helped with that."

"Well, if that failed, my backup plan was guilt."

Jackson grinned. "Thanksgiving is in a week. We only have five more weeks to finish the remodel."

"I know. Duncan's been working around the clock, keeping up with things at the Calypso. I check in on him every morning and evening."

Jackson hesitated before meeting her gaze. "Molly, I think it's time you get back to your *own* work. I've got things covered here. You're not much help on the work site, and you've already handled all the paperwork. If you stay, you're spinning your wheels. But if you're at the Calypso, you can actually be useful."

"I help! I even have a pink hard hat." Molly sighed and crossed her arms, surveying the bustling center. "I'd rather stay here...but you're right. The hard part is done. Volunteers are stepping up left and right. We've got painters working on the classrooms, an electrician rewiring the entire building with better lighting and additional power outlets, and a plumber fixing every leaky sink in the kitchen and bathrooms. In a way, the fire may have been one of the best things to happen to this place. It reminded people how important it is."

"Well, I'm proud of you for helping them see that."

Molly looked at Jackson and shrugged. "My contractor was distracted. It was the least I could do."

"Sure, that's the story we'll go with."

Molly couldn't stay away. As soon as the weekend gave her a break from her Calypso duties, she turned up bright and early at the community center.

She'd looked forward to the smiling faces all week. Every day, Jackson and his helpers checked new items off the list, and watching the community come together to make them happen was nothing short of inspiring.

The center was a melting pot of ages, heritages, and histories. Whether struggling, thriving, young, old, a native, or new to Serenity, everyone shared a sense of welcome that made this place feel like home.

Perched on a stool in the classroom, Molly painted the wall a soft robin's egg blue. A little boy in a wheelchair watched her work, grinning. "Don't forget that corner over there!"

She flicked a bit of paint in his direction with a smirk. "Keep it up, and I'll give you a brush, too."

"You wouldn't," he teased. "I'd out-paint you for sure. You're scared I'd beat you."

When his mom walked into the room, Molly had already given in, letting him paint pictures of flowers and smiley faces before she rolled a fresh coat over them.

"Hey, thanks for keeping me company," she told him as he rolled toward the door.

The boy grinned. "I'll be back tomorrow!"

"Great! We'll be painting the next room green."

"Can you do one red? That's my favorite color."

Molly shook her head and said, "Let me see what Jackson thinks."

"Bye, Ms. Molly!"

"Bye, Richie."

Once he left, the hum of the center settled around her. Distant strains of recorders squeaking through "Hot Cross Buns" filled the halls, mixing with the chatter of mothers tending to fussy babies. Her stomach rumbled, reminding her she hadn't eaten since early that morning. She set the roller on the paint tray and headed to the kitchen to find food.

She'd expected a crowd of people, but not a flood. People scrambled back and forth, passing pots and bowls while water poured over the edges of the sink like a broken dam.

"What happened?" she asked, rushing inside.

"I don't know! It wouldn't turn off. The faucet keeps spinning."

Ducking under the sink, Molly reached for the water shut-off valve. These kinds of problems were second nature after years of living in a too-cheap, barely functional apartment during college.

"Call Jackson," she said to the nearest person, passing off her phone. "His number's in my recent calls."

By the time Jackson arrived twenty minutes later, the water had stopped, but the aftermath remained—sopping towels piled high, a sink still filled to the brim with murky water, and the occasional stray splash hitting the floor.

"Gertie, I thought the plumber signed off on everything," Jackson said, running his hand through his hair as he stepped into the mess.

"He did," the older woman said, shaking her head. "It was fine, and then suddenly it wasn't."

He tested the knobs and twisted the faucet handles before he sighed. "Looks like a bad faucet."

Molly couldn't help but notice how his white button-up clung to his chest when he rolled his sleeves up and reached into the sink. When he pulled out the drain plug and turned, she could see through the thin fabric where water soaked the front of his shirt.

"What?" she said, hands raised.

He raised an amused eyebrow at her.

"I showed up, and it was already like this."

Gertie wrung out the towel in her hands. "I'm sorry, Mr. Beaumont. With the water pouring everywhere, I didn't even think about the drain. I just panicked."

"How'd you stop the water?"

"Ms. Molly crawled under there and turned it off."

Jackson's smile nearly knocked the breath from her lungs. Combined with the way his water soaked shirt clung to his muscles, it was enough to leave her lightheaded.

"Good thinking, Molly," he praised. "Let's see if I can't get this fixed."

It didn't take long for him to diagnose the problem. The whole time, as he lay beneath the sink, tinkering with valves and twisting fittings, Molly couldn't help but admire him. Jackson made things look effortless—and more importantly, he made them work.

After twenty minutes, he wiped his hands and declared, "Looks like the plumber installed a faulty valve. It's not common, but it happens. I'll call him. Thank God this wasn't a bathroom or anywhere near the kids. I doubt they'd have been such quick thinkers."

She chuckled. "Thanks for playing the hero, Jackson."

"It was nothing. You'd already saved yourself. I only helped clean up the mess."

That was Jackson for you...casual, capable, and just impossible enough to ignore.

"How are things at the Calypso?" she asked.

"Better than here. The ground floor's nearly done. The crew's been rotating through rooms all week, the exterior's getting painted, and the landscaper is coming by the end of the week."

Relief washed over her. "Jackson, you don't *know* what a weight off my shoulders that is." She exhaled, pushing her hands through her hair. "We're making substantial progress here too, aside from today's waterworks. Every day, we find something new, but I know this place will never be perfect. It's hard to walk away knowing there's more to do."

Jackson watched her carefully as she spoke, his eyes flickering with something unreadable.

She kept going, determined to focus. "Some moms and I were talking about fixing up the playground in the back. The equipment is rusty and breaking down. I'm planning to start a fundraiser next week. Then I was thinking we could organize a Christmas play with the kids. Something fun to wrap up the end of the year...what?" She stopped mid-sentence. "You're looking at me funny."

"It sounds like you're settling in," he said, his voice softer now. "I thought you were heading home once the Calypso was done."

Her fingers traced the rim of the kitchen sink as she hesitated. "I am." But even as she said it, the words felt...off.

For the first time, she allowed herself to ask what she truly wanted. It wasn't the promotion, or polishing her resume with a new, shiny hotel.

It was the warm, undeniable safety of Jackson's arms. The simplicity of bringing their *kids* to the community center to learn ballet or play soccer. It was Christmas carols and cookies and watching little ones on stage.

"It was just a thought. You're right." She swallowed hard. "This place will still have you when I'm gone."

Over the next two days, she distracted herself by staying in her hotel room with paperwork. She didn't call Ana. She didn't check in at the community center. The only person she spoke to was Paul.

His praise felt like water in a desert. He reminded her that the *actual* goal, the *real* reason she was here, was the promotion. His encouragement grounded her, gave her purpose.

Jackson?

Jackson is a temptation. A voice whispered that success wasn't the only thing worth chasing.

It wasn't until she woke up on Thanksgiving morning, finding her inbox empty, that she remembered it was a holiday. The hotel room felt smaller, the bed emptier.

Her phone buzzed.

Early dinner at three. You coming? Bring pie.

The screen held her gaze, fingers hovering.

Falling for everything Jackson had built was tempting, and stopping herself felt...undesirable.

After waiting a moment, she typed back:

What sort of pie?

Chapter Twenty

Molly

No one heard her knock on the door, so she let herself into Jackson's house. Instead of the warm greeting she'd hoped for, she silently slipped in and observed the group of family and friends from afar.

Marco and Duncan were in front of the large TV, animatedly arguing over a football play. Ana was helping one of Jackson's crew members set the table, while Jackson himself stood shoulder to shoulder with Jessica in the kitchen, chopping vegetables.

A weight settled in Molly's stomach.

She recognized Jessica immediately—the doctor Jackson had mentioned more than once. A longtime friend, he'd said. Someone who'd been around for years.

And yet, watching them laugh together, the familiarity between them felt intimate in a way Molly hadn't expected.

Uncomfortable and suddenly out of place, she watched the two of them. The sight reminded her—painfully—that Jackson wasn't hers. And even if she had a choice, Texas wasn't her home.

She carefully set the pie down on the small table near the door. Her fingers grazed the doorknob when a familiar voice called out.

"Ms. Monroe! Sure is good to see you."

She plastered a smile on her face and turned. "Hey, Duncan. How've you been?"

"Good," he said, grinning. "We've missed you at the job site. We still have your pink hat waiting for you."

She said, "I'll be by soon, I promise."

"Is that pumpkin pie?"

"No, it's Pecan."

"Even better. Come on in!"

The bustling house, filled with laughter and conversation, transported her back. She remembered quiet moments spent sitting by candlelight, talking to Jackson. Now, on top of having fantasies about playing with their children, she imagined what else they could have. Her mind had betrayed her with images of future family-filled holidays, crowded game nights, and football Sundays.

She recognized Marco immediately, even though they'd only met twice. He stood near Ana, holding a beer, watching the game. Across the room, Jackson wrapped his arms around Jessica. The doctor leaned in to rest her head on his shoulder as he whispered something in her ear. With a laugh, they parted. Jessica began cutting carrots on the board, while Jackson turned to grab something from the fridge.

Molly took a step back, turning toward the door. She

reached for the knob, but Ana's voice stopped her.

"Leaving so soon? Where are you running off to?"

"Anywhere but here." She glanced over her shoulder toward the kitchen. "I think coming was a bad idea."

Ana followed her gaze to watch the two in the kitchen. "They're only friends, you know."

Molly swallowed hard. "Honestly, I don't know. No one ever told me otherwise."

"I'm telling you now." Ana looked back towards the kitchen. "They might have made it once, but they didn't know what they were losing. I think Jackson's learned his lesson and Jess, well, she's more clear on what she wants, now, but the damage is done."

Together, Ana and Molly watched Jessica and Jackson working side by side. The doctor rubbed her eyes and spoke to Jackson, who cupped her face in his hands and smiled at her.

Ana smirked. "Lord, girl, did your teeth just crack?"

Molly swore under her breath as Jackson started turning in their direction. Her fingers clenched the doorknob as his voice called out.

"Hey, you made it!"

She froze.

Jackson brushed his hands on a kitchen towel and strode toward her.

Ana gave her a wink before retreating to Marco's side, leaving Molly standing awkwardly near the entrance.

"Apparently, pie is a hot commodity on Thanksgiving," she said, forcing a light tone. "I had to go to two grocery stores before I found what you wanted."

Jackson arched an eyebrow. "But you got pecan, right?"

She laughed at his look of horror. "Right, because 'pumpkin pie is for losers,'" she said, making air quotes.

"Phew. I was worried for a second. Marco insisted on pumpkin, so Ana betrayed me. It's not Thanksgiving without the king of desserts."

"Yeah, I'm sure you were suffering."

Jackson smirked, taking the pie from her and setting it aside, then stepping closer. He engulfed her in a hug, and whispered in her ear, "I'm glad you could be here. I missed you."

She gave him a quick squeeze before stepping back, her eyes darting around before settling on him. "Thanks for having me. It looks like you invited everyone."

Following her gaze, Jackson sighed. "Jessica always spends the holidays here. She doesn't have any family in town, and... well, they're not the kind worth traveling to see."

Molly nodded stiffly. "I'm glad she has you." She forced a neutral expression, pushing down the jealousy.

"Come on, I'll introduce you properly. Last time you talked to her, you were heavily medicated."

Molly groaned. "So embarrassing." She ran a hand over her face. "I should thank her for taking good care of me, though."

As they entered the kitchen, Jackson gently placed a hand on Jessica's shoulder. "Jess, do you remember Molly?"

Jessica turned, offering a warm smile. "Of course." She extended a hand. "You look like you recovered well."

"I had a brilliant doctor," Molly said with a wink.

"Thanks." Jessica laughed, and said, "I'm just finishing up the salad before dinner."

Molly hesitated. "Can I help?"

"Sure, but there's not much left to do."

Jackson grinned. "Since you have an extra hand, I'm going to see if Marco needs help frying the turkey."

"Be careful, I'm not offering emergency services on a holiday...."

Jack winked and left.

With him gone, the kitchen fell into a comfortable rhythm. Jessica occasionally handed Molly vegetables to chop or wash, while the steady hum of voices and TV commentary filled the space. The quiet between them stretched until Jessica said, "I know this is probably a little weird."

Molly exhaled. "A little. I don't know what Jackson told you, but we aren't dating."

Jessica nodded. "He sort of implied that you were...undefined."

Molly let out a dry laugh. "Honestly, that's probably the best way to put it."

Jessica turned toward her. "I just don't want things to be uncomfortable for you. Jackson's been looking out for me for years. He knows holidays can be tough."

Molly gave a small nod. "I get that." She paused, considering her words. "I guess I'm having trouble sorting my life out. And with Jackson, I seem to be chronically uncomfortable." She smirked. "I might qualify as a stray, too."

Jessica grinned. "So, what's your story?"

"I work in property development—normally based in Seattle, but I'm here on a project. Jackson is my contractor."

"Interesting," Jessica said. "He appears to be handling more than most contractors do."

"Right." Molly chuckled. "He may be a little more than my contractor."

Jessica asked, "Kind of like how I used to be a little more than his doctor?"

Molly's interest piqued. "You could tell me about that."

"We were together for a while—a few years. He wanted a family, wanted to settle down, and I wasn't ready. Not that he's not a great guy, but I couldn't bring a kid into the life I had growing up." Jessica hesitated a moment before shrugging. "Of course, later on, I realized that our child's life wouldn't be anything like mine, but by then...the damage was done." She shook her head. "We said some pretty harsh things, and in the long run, we realized we were better off as friends. Now, he's more like an older brother."

Molly processed that. "It must've been hard, becoming a doctor. Lots of commitment and sacrifice."

"Exactly. Back then, I thought I couldn't have both—a career and a family. It took some growing up to realize balance is possible."

"I worry about that too. My ex, Mitchell, treated them as mutually exclusive."

Jessica offered a knowing smile. "Balancing both is hard, but Jackson and I learned a lot from each other. I realized I want a family someday, and he—well, he learned some women value ambition just as much as he values roots."

"Sounds like you two found mutual respect."

Jessica nodded. "It only took us breaking up to get there!"

By the end of their conversation, Molly had decided that

she really liked Jessica. They opened a bottle of wine, toasted to their exes, and finished cooking in the kitchen. "Honestly, even though we are...undefined, I have to admit that I was a little jealous of you and Jackson."

"I figured, but I didn't want you to be."

"I'm glad that we could work out being friends."

"Me too," said Molly as she grabbed a bowl of potatoes with two hot pads.

While she was walking the food to the table, Jackson stopped her. "The turkey's about ready. Need help getting set up?"

"No, I think Jess and I have it handled."

His eyes twinkled. "You two seem to get along well."

"She's pretty amazing," Molly admitted.

"Don't let her tell you any lies about me."

She grinned and brushed past him. "Too late. She already told me about your 'incident' in Cancún."

"All lies," he called after her. "I had food poisoning, and it was a public place."

"Sure..." Molly said and walked away laughing as Jessica and Jackson fell into playful bickering behind her.

Chapter Twenty-One

Jackson

Jackson glanced toward the archway leading from the kitchen. There was a faint shift in the air, just enough to raise the hairs on his neck. A sixth sense, honed from job sites and gut instincts, told him before his eyes did. She was here.

Framed by the threshold, haloed by the afternoon light falling through the glass, stood Molly. Jackson's chest tightened, heart giving a sudden, sharp kick against his ribs.

Jessica hadn't noticed. She was elbow deep in onions, laughing at a joke he'd barely heard, although he'd nodded along like his mind hadn't just imploded.

But now Molly stood there with her big blue eyes, uncertain and wide enough to pierce through him. Legs braced like she might bolt any second, sweater clutched a little too tightly, curls half-wild from the humidity outside, but she hadn't run yet.

His fingers tightened around the knife handle. Not from anger, not even nerves. It was gratitude. Mouth dry, his pulse tripping like he hadn't already played out this moment a hundred times in his head and none of those versions included her actually staying.

Ana had beaten him to the door, of course. He owed her a bonus, or, at least, some flowers. She was already mid-whisper with Molly. He hoped it wouldn't drive her back out the door.

From the stove, Jessica bumped his shoulder. She just smirked down into her pan, like she knew where his brain was. And hell, she probably did. Exes who weren't enemies read you as if you hadn't changed, even when you had.

He wiped his hands on a towel and counted to ten. It was the only thing keeping him from looking too desperate and rushing to the door.

Ana laughed. Thank God. Molly cracked a small smile. The curve of her lip was barely there, but it was real. Her shoulders loosened. She looked his way.

And, didn't that just sucker-punch him?

He took a breath and stated to walk towards her. Measured. Purposeful. He knew if he startled her she'd leave again. Eventually, he wouldn't be able to convince her to come back.

"Hey," he said, his voice pitching low. "You finally made it."

She met his eyes, soft and cautious.

"Got your pie," she said, lifting one shoulder, like she wasn't sure if he'd still want it...or her.

Before he could overthink it, he wrapped his arms around her. "I'm glad you could be here," he said. Something in his throat snagged. "I missed you."

Hers was a quick squeeze. Maybe it didn't say forever, but it didn't say goodbye either.

He'd take that.

They stepped apart and her eyes did what hers always did in a crowded room: scan, assess, and measure her place in it. He followed her eyes to the kitchen where Jessica rolled dough like she had something to prove to the Food Network. The two of them? They were years and miles in the rearview mirror. There was no judgment Molly's stare, just curiosity. Those gears in her head were always turning.

"Thanks for having me," she said, pulling her gaze back to him. "Looks like you invited everyone." There was a weight in Molly's voice when she said, "I'm glad she has you."

It wasn't a loaded statement, but the note in it?

Sharp.

Explaining wouldn't help, not when the tension still clung to her like static. Instead, he leaned in slightly. "Come on, I'll introduce you two properly."

Jackson walked her into the kitchen, kept his pace easy, and only let his shoulder brush against her once. Catching Jessica's attention, he said, "You remember Molly." His voice even though every nerve in him was waiting to see what would happen.

"Of course," Jessica said with that grin she gave a patient after a clean bill of health. "You look like you recovered well."

"Thanks to a brilliant doctor," Molly said, her smile tight around the edges, but genuine.

Polite. Friendly. Not warm, but something passed between them. A thread of relief, maybe. Acceptance. Or at least mutual confirmation that neither one was going to draw blood.

Good.

He felt himself breathe again. Jackson backed out before

Molly could cool, nodding toward the porch. "I'm going to help Marco fry the turkey."

It was a lie. The turkey didn't need help. He just needed five minutes to pull himself together.

Outside, the fryer hissed like it had a vendetta, and Jackson grabbed a beer from the cooler, popping the top with the edge of the patio table.

Across the deck, Marco admitted to Duncan he didn't know what a holding call was. Neither one appeared to care about roasting the bird.

"You good?" Marco asked, flicking an eye toward the house.

"Getting there," Jackson said, lifting the bottle in a silent toast.

Inside, through the kitchen window, he could see Molly was still by Jessica's side. Was she laughing? Dammit, she was laughing.

He knew that sound. It was the one he lived for.

He wondered if she'd eat the pie. If she'd help set the table. Whether she'd sleep through the Cowboys game or narrate the foul plays just to make him mad and get his attention.

Would she stay?

Don't get greedy, he warned himself. She was here. That was more than he'd dared ask for this morning. Since she left, Jackson had thought about it; he didn't need a declaration or a promise. Not even a kiss. He just needed enough time to show her what he could give her: a warm kitchen, loud laughter, too much butter, and not enough grace.

It wasn't flashy, but it was real. It was a home.

Chapter Twenty-Two

Molly

Platters, bowls, and casserole dishes filled with food covered the table. Jackson had cooked a fifteen-pound turkey, Duncan had brought his mama's famous stuffing recipe, and Ana and Marco arrived with a spicy pumpkin soup. Jessica had perfected rich, buttery mashed potatoes. Extras and sides filled every remaining inch of the table.

"I'd like to thank everyone for being here today." Jackson raised his glass for a toast. "I am truly blessed to have each of you in my life. Every single one of you adds something unique to my world. And on this day, as we reflect on what we're thankful for, I want you all to know that I'm thankful for you."

"Here, here!"

"Cheers!"

The room erupted in agreement, with excited claps and murmurs of appreciation. Jackson glanced across the table, his gaze locking with Molly's. He smiled and said, "To those joining us for the first time, welcome. For those of you who have been here before, you know the rules. Use your manners, avoid the boarding house reach, and dig in!"

Laughter rippled through the group as serving bowls and plates passed around the table. Molly accepted and passed every dish handed to her until there was a food mountain on her plate.

Across the table, Jessica caught her eye and grinned. "Do your best," she teased with a wink.

Ana, seated beside Molly, nudged her. "You look over-whelmed."

"A little," Molly admitted. "We never had meals like this at home. It was always me, my mom, and my dad for the holidays. By the time I got to high school, my parents had given up on celebrating altogether. They said it wasn't worth the effort for such a small group. Normally, we took family vacations, or ate out, for the holidays."

"Really?" Ana asked, surprised.

"I guess it made sense," said Molly. "There's so much food."

"Yes!" Marco interjected with a playful smirk. "And, we're going to eat it!"

When everyone had a full belly, Molly looked around the table at what was left. They'd made a pretty decent dent in the mounds of food.

Jessica handed Molly a stack of to-go containers. "This way, everyone has something for lunch tomorrow."

They worked side-by-side packing up the food. Duncan was the first guest to grab a container of leftovers, then Marco and Ana swung by, too.

"Jessica?" Molly hesitated before continuing. "I wanted to apologize for earlier."

Jessica turned to her, offering a small smile. "You're not the first to be confused by Mr. Jackson Beaumont, dear."

After they'd handed off the last of the containers to the crew, Jackson approached and rested a hand on Jessica's shoulder.

"Thanks for coming tonight."

"It's always a pleasure, Jack. But I have to head out soon. I'm covering the late shift at the clinic. I promised the on-call nurse she'd get some time with her family, and it sounds like it's been busy there."

Jackson laughed. "I can see how turkey carving could be dangerous work."

Molly and Jackson waved goodbye to Ana, Marco, and Jessica as they left with their arms full of food.

They were finally alone.

Jackson turned toward her, hesitated, and asked, "I can give you a ride back to your hotel, but..." Slowly, he lifted a hand, brushing a stray piece of hair away from her face. "Can we talk for a bit?"

Before she could answer, he gently took her hand and led her to the couch, pulling her onto his lap as he sat down.

"I've missed having you here," he said.

"I've missed being here," she admitted softly.

"Then why don't you come back?"

The house had settled into a comfortable quiet after the day's festivities. It felt different from her hotel where she could hear the hum of traffic and the familiar rhythm of the city. Here, nestled against Jackson in his quiet living room, she felt a warmth surrounding her.

She leaned back against the couch arm, resting her hand on his chest. Beneath her fingers, his heartbeat was steady and strong.

"Can we light a candle?" she asked, twisting the fabric of his shirt between her fingers.

Jackson smiled. "Of course."

When the small flame flickered to life, a soft glow filled the room. Shadows danced across the walls, wrapping them in quiet warmth.

"When I'm here, everything else fades away," she said. "The problem isn't *us*—it's *this*."

"What's wrong with this?" he asked, his thumb tracing a gentle line down her arm.

"You know what. This risks the job. It's everything I've worked toward for years."

He studied her for a moment before nodding. "I know, Molly. I just hate seeing you fight so hard."

"It's only been a recent struggle," she said quietly. "For years I thought if I worked hard enough, they'd see how much I contributed. I liked it."

Jackson's expression softened. "I'm not sure they ever did. But what you've done with the Calypso Hotel is incredible. We've done so much."

"We?" she echoed, a small smile curving her lips. "I like that."

He slipped an arm around her, drawing her gently against

him. "Stay here tonight," he murmured against her hair.

"I don't think I can," she admitted, though her voice wavered. "You're too easy to get used to."

"I've been trying to fight it since the first day." His fingers brushed through her hair, tender, searching. "You were full of fire, but you had a spark I couldn't ignore."

She laughed softly, the sound catching in her throat. "You feel too good to be around. Staying here with you might be a bad idea."

He smiled against her temple. "We've tried being apart...that wasn't such a good idea either."

She swallowed hard.

For a long moment, neither of them moved. Her pulse beat against his palm; his breath stirred her hair. Everything they weren't saying seemed to hang in the still air between them.

"Molly," he whispered, his voice unsteady.

She looked up, eyes luminous in the candlelight. "I know."

He brushed his thumb across her cheek, then leaned in until their foreheads touched. The world outside disappeared.

"I'm not ready to leave, yet," she said, the words barely more than breath.

Jackson's reply came as a whisper against her lips. "Then don't."

Their mouths met—slow, certain, full of everything they'd both been holding back. The kiss deepened until words no longer mattered, until the room seemed to hum with the quiet promise between them.

Chapter Twenty-Three

Molly

Her hands trembled as she slid her palms down Jackson's arms, feeling the warmth beneath his rolled-up sleeves. Their fingers intertwined, and the frantic rush between them finally stilled.

For a long heartbeat, neither moved. The air between them seemed to hum with everything left unsaid. Then she took a slow step forward, close enough that the space between them disappeared.

"Tell me to stop," she whispered.

His voice came out rough. "I can't. I don't want to."

Something inside her shifted at the honesty in his tone. She reached for him, and he rose to meet her, his hands finding hers as if he'd been waiting a long time to do so.

The world narrowed to a shared breath, a shared heartbeat. When their eyes met, the moment broke open, and she leaned in. Their lips met in a kiss that was gentle and certain, filled with everything they hadn't dared to say aloud. It wasn't hurried. It was the kind of kiss that changed something quietly and permanently.

When they finally drew apart, his hands were still clasped around hers. "You sure about this?" he asked, his voice soft, steady.

"One night," she said, her voice barely above a whisper. "That's all I can promise."

He nodded slowly, his thumb brushing over her knuckles. "Then that will have to be enough."

Molly swallowed hard, the ache in her chest sharp and sweet all at once. She kissed him again, and the world seemed to blur at the edges—everything slipping into warmth and shadow.

When Jackson stirred sometime later, soft light from the street lamp spilled across the room, catching the faint outline of her hair against the pillow. Molly lay beside him, her breathing slow and even.

For a long moment, he just watched her—half afraid that if he blinked, she'd disappear.

"You okay?" he whispered.

A tired smile curved her lips. "Better than."

The silence between them wasn't awkward. It was quiet, full, content. For once, she didn't feel the need to fill it.

The muted glow from outside painted soft golden bars across his face, and she turned slightly toward him, studying the way the light touched his jaw, the easy rhythm of his breathing.

"You gonna run away again?" he asked, breaking the hush.

"Probably," she admitted. "But I don't want to."

His throat bobbed as he swallowed, eyes searching hers.

She kissed the tip of his nose—soft, almost adoring—then rolled away to make some space. His arm slipped around her waist, pulling her back.

"For the record," he murmured, voice scratchy with sleep and something heavier, "best Thanksgiving ever."

She laughed quietly and settled against him, memorizing the steady beat of his heart and the warmth of his breath in her hair.

Later, when his breathing deepened, she whispered, "You asleep?"

No response.

She watched him for a long moment, wanting him to wake—to make the choice she wasn't ready to make herself. Instead, careful not to disturb him, she eased away, his hand falling loosely from her hip.

She pulled on her sweater, then her boots, wincing when a floorboard creaked. Every sound felt too loud in the still room, her pulse thudding in her ears.

At the door, she hesitated.

Jackson lay peaceful beneath the dim light, one arm thrown over his head, mouth soft and unguarded. It struck her then how easily she could fit here—and how dangerous that thought was.

He'd be frustrated when morning came and she wasn't there. He'd pretend not to be, and she'd pretend not to notice.

Staying was too hard. Staying meant words she wasn't ready to say and choices she wasn't ready to make. It meant laying her ambition beside his open heart and hoping neither broke.

She closed the door softly behind her.

Outside, the night air was cool against her skin as she crossed the yard toward her car, parked where she'd left it earlier that evening. The familiar weight of the keys in her hand grounded her more than she expected.

She slid into the driver's seat and rested her hands on the steering wheel, forcing herself not to look back.

The engine sounded too loud as it turned over. She pulled away slowly, the porch light fading in the rearview mirror as she headed toward the road—and the choices waiting for her in the morning.

She hugged her arms around herself, willing her pulse to slow, telling her head to be louder than her heart.

Just until morning.

Chapter Twenty-Four

Jackson

"Where are you? You aren't here."

Jackson stared at the tangled sheets where she'd been the night before—the faint smell of her still clinging to the cotton. He lifted his phone from the side table, sighing before dialing.

"Grabbing coffee at Patty's" Her voice was light and teasing. "I needed extra caffeine to get moving after a late night."

"Why do you keep disappearing when I'm sleeping? You're going to give me insomnia, or something."

"Whatever, you filled up on turkey and took a holiday nap," she said. "You did look super cute, all scrunched up and drooling on yourself."

"I don't drool," he grumbled, trying to keep the edge out of his voice.

"Maybe not, but you do snore."

He leaned back against the headboard, rubbing a hand over his chest. It wasn't what she said, it was what she didn't. No apology. No explanation. Just a soft smile in her voice, like nothing had changed.

Jackson tried to smirk, but a tight knot twisted somewhere behind his ribs. He could practically picture her at Patty Cakes—as natural in that old café as if she'd lived in Serenity for years. She probably had her curls piled on top of her head, eyes still puffy from sleep, stirring way too much creamer into her coffee, and flashing that look that made his knees weak and his resolve weaker.

He could see Candy leaning in close, refilling Molly's cup like she belonged there. That was the cruelest part—she did. She belonged here more than she did in Seattle. She didn't have anyone there that *really* cared about her.

"I was thinking about stopping by the job site this morning," she said.

The tension in his shoulders loosened a little. "I'm sure Duncan would love to see you," he said, keeping his tone easy. "I was heading to the community center."

To her, it was a schedule update. To him, it felt like hope. She hadn't closed the door. Not completely.

"Then I'll meet you there afterwards. I've been curious about how things are going,"

Jackson smiled, letting himself imagine her stepping under the awning of the fresh, painted community center. He already pictured her eyes lighting up at the sight of the kids, and fighting to pretend the tiniest upgrade didn't impress her.

"Well, I have a surprise for you," he said, hearing the mischief creep into his voice like second nature. "Message me when you're on your way."

He ended the call, and let the phone rest on his chest,

staring at the ceiling. For a moment, he pretended this could work. That it would last beyond a stolen night.

He'd waited once before. Waited with Jessica, ignored the signs, the distance, the shallow "later" promises. He kept telling himself she'd come around, that they'd align one day.

And they never did.

Molly was fire and ambition, a woman who didn't beg for love because she didn't need it to define her. That mattered to him. Didn't it? He knew he'd messed it up with Jess, but he wanted to give Molly everything she needed to thrive, but he knew he needed to be honest, too. *Honest with himself.*

Now, there were mornings like this, quiet, half-empty ones, where he stared down the length of his house and wondered what it would feel like to fill it with chairs too small for grown-ups, walls covered in crayon art and growth charts scratched into the kitchen doorframe. He wanted roots. A backyard mess. A forever. And maybe part of him hoped Molly would come to want that, too.

But she always left.

He wouldn't push her. Not again. Love wasn't supposed to be something you could force someone into. It was enough...or it wasn't.

Still, as he stood and began pulling on his boots with her voice clinging to the edges of his thoughts, he hoped.

Just once, he wished she'd reach for more than the door.

Chapter Twenty-Five

Molly

Molly couldn't speak. She stood, slowly rotating in the lobby until she was too dizzy to continue.

"You guys did all of this?"

"Yes, ma'am. Mr. Beaumont pulled in some temp help and has had the crews working day and night."

"It's gorgeous." Molly looked up at the chrome and glass chandelier illuminating the entrance, then walked to the receptionist's counter, savoring the sharp click of her boots on white-and-silver-flecked granite tiles. She ran her hand along the smooth chrome edge, stopping at the large aquarium.

"There aren't any fish in it yet. We thought you'd like to help pick them out."

"Neon," she said. "They'll pop against that black wall. With LED strip lighting, they'll glow even brighter. We should see if we can get some." Pivoting on her heels, she grinned. "Can I see a bedroom?"

"Sure," Duncan said. "Most of the guest rooms are ready.

We're spending extra time finishing the luxury suites."

Room after room left her in awe. Even the simplest accommodations had a touch of magic. Cozy sitting nooks framed panoramic views, while bathrooms showcased elegant glass fixtures and top-of-the-line toiletries. The soft down comforters and throws covering the beds in various pastels, jewel tones, and metallics were her favorite feature.

Every floor had a theme, yet the transitions were seamless. Unless someone explored each level, they'd never guess the hotel offered both refined luxury suites and peaceful, spa-like quarters. The Calypso had something for everyone.

"We'll have the landscaping and exterior completed soon," Duncan said.

Molly turned to him, overwhelmed with gratitude. "Duncan, I don't have enough words to express how amazing this is. What you and the crew have done...it's just short of miraculous."

"Well, Ms. Molly, I will pass that along. There's still plenty to do, and it motivates the guys to know they're getting it right. We have house staff in for training we're working around, too. There are lots of excited people helping out."

"They're doing a phenomenal job," she assured him. "I'll let you get back to it, but thank you for showing me around today. I've got a photographer coming soon. We still need to set up a website and update the promo materials."

"Just let me know what you need."

On impulse, she threw her arms around the surprised foreman in a bone-crushing hug. "Oh, thank you!"

A wave of exhilaration swept over her, and she couldn't resist swinging by the community center to check on Jackson's progress. She was leaning out of her car window before she'd even fully parked, eyes wide with excitement.

"Blue! You painted it blue!"

In the parking lot, Jackson turned with a knowing grin. "I remember—it's your second-favorite color, right after green."

After paying the driver and hopping out, she ran straight to him, flinging herself into his arms and spinning him in giddy circles.

"Not that I'm complaining," he teased, "but what's this for?"

"I'm in a hugging mood."

"Well, come back here, then! I'm in the mood, too."

She laughed and kept walking toward the painters covering the old, faded cream walls with sapphire blue and white accents.

Jackson stepped behind her, lowering his voice as he said, "It's the color of your eyes."

"You can't paint an entire building the color of my eyes," she protested, spinning back into his arms.

"No, but I can paint *this* wall," he said, "then use neutral browns and creams for the rest. We've even got a mural planned."

She shook her head. "How do you always manage to be *that* guy?"

His expression softened. "Because I see you."

Her pulse skipped. "I don't think I can resist you much

longer."

"Then don't."

"But what happens when I stop?"

Jackson's lips quirked into a slow smile. "Maybe we just enjoy the ride?"

The Texas sun warmed her skin as she leaned up on her toes and kissed him. But before she had time to savor it—

"Hey! Excuse me."

Jackson turned. "Yes?"

A man in a crisp button-down extended his hand. "I'm with *The Houston Chronicle.* I'd like to interview the contractor in charge of the site."

"That's me," Jackson said, shaking his hand.

"Oh, pardon me." The reporter smiled. "I've been hearing great things about this project. We'd love to feature it in an upcoming piece. Perhaps you'd like the publicity?"

Molly stepped back and smiled as she caught Jackson's eye. Before he could protest, she turned to the reporter. "He'd be happy to talk with you." With a quick wave, she walked away, ignoring Jackson's exasperated look.

Pulling out her phone, she sent him a quick text: *It's good for you. <3 :**

As she pulled out of the lot, her phone dinged. She glanced in the rearview mirror and saw Jackson looking down at his own phone.

Call me later...I want to wake up next to you.

✺

Back at the hotel, Molly's fingers shook as she dialed Paul.

"Molly," he said, "how's everything coming along?"

"It's amazing, Paul. I visited the Calypso today. I'm sure we'll be ready when you and Mr. Maherson arrive in a couple of weeks. We're right on track for the grand opening."

"I can't wait to check it out," Paul said. "I've been keeping Mr. Maherson updated, and he's as excited as I am. It's going to be an unforgettable weekend."

"Working on this project with you has been incredible."

"You deserve every bit of what's coming your way."

"That means a lot," said Molly. "Can you have Conner send me your travel itinerary?"

"Of course. He's been a big help recently. The NorthStart guests will be staying at the Calypso when we arrive?"

"Naturally. We'll make sure you have the best accommodations."

Her pen hovered over the paper in front of her. Lists upon lists—plans, details, final touches. The upcoming gala had to be flawless.

When Ana knocked, Molly barely glanced up. "Come in!"

The lock beeped, and Ana backed through the door, arms stacked with boxes.

"Let me help! What's all this?"

"I figured you could use some help." Ana winked. "The locals sent samples—food, centerpieces, printed materials. We need to pick vendors."

Molly grinned. "Have I ever told you I love you?"

Ana smirked. "Only that one time we were drinking."

Molly's eyes widened as she lifted a glossy pamphlet from a box. "Is this...the Calypso?" She traced the vibrant photo in awe. "I hardly recognize it."

"I had Duncan snap some pictures and sent it to test print quality. Once the professional photographer's photos are ready, it'll be even better."

Molly pulled out an elongated chrome bowl, laser-etched with the hotel's logo. "This is incredible."

"I thought they'd make great centerpieces. Add flowers, subtle lighting, and after the party, they can be re-purposed throughout the hotel."

"Ana, have you thought of *everything*?"

"Obviously."

Molly grabbed another box, pulling it open. A warm, spicy aroma filled the room.

"What is *this*?"

Ana grinned. "Dinner! The caterer prepped samples for the proposed menu. Chipotle cornbread and chili. Fancy name, basic concept. A deconstructed Texas barbecue—plated elegantly. This is the soup and bread course."

Molly took a bite, savoring the rich, smoky flavor. "I love it all..." She hesitated.

Ana watched her closely, and asked, "What?"

Molly set the spoon down and exhaled. "You were my first friend here. You and Duncan...if not for you two, I might have killed Jackson by now."

"He's a good guy," laughed Ana. "His heart's in the right

place."

"He is, isn't he?"

Ana nudged her. "It's obvious there's something there. He's interested, but he's giving you space. *You* keep pretending you don't need him."

"I *don't* need a man."

"There's a difference between needing and *wanting*. He softens you. You test him. You're from different worlds, but you make each other better."

Molly focused on her chili. "I'll miss food like this when I go home."

Ana went still.

"You'll visit, right?" Molly swallowed. "Someone has to check in on the Calypso."

"Sure," Ana said. "But big business doesn't wait forever."

The night passed with paperwork, planning, and samples. By the time Ana left, Molly's to-do list had doubled, but she was humming with excitement for the big unveiling.

She was jotting notes when Jackson texted her.

Dinner tonight?

Sorry, ate with Ana. Lots to do. Maybe another time?

We're running out of time.

Yeah, we are.

The silence that followed felt heavy. Ignoring him felt cruel, but leaning in felt impossible. She turned off her phone and lay in the dark. Thoughts came and went, but sleep was slow to arrive.

Chapter Twenty-Six

Molly

She was avoiding him.

Jackson.

At first, it was easy enough—burying herself in work, claiming she was too busy to talk. Then came the unanswered texts, the calls she let ring out. Now, she couldn't even look at her phone without feeling that familiar pulse of guilt.

How did you tell someone they were the best thing that had ever happened to you—but that you couldn't do it anymore? That the feelings were real, just not strong enough to survive the reality of them?

The truth was, she was interested. Just not enough to risk ruining everything.

As the launch date crept closer—weeks shrinking into days—she drowned herself in logistics: schedules, vendor calls, endless checklists for the gala event. Work was a perfect anesthetic. The busier she stayed, the less she thought about Jackson. Or what she'd left behind at his house.

When the knock came, it barely registered at first. She was too deep in an email thread, halfway through typing a response she wouldn't remember sending. Then another knock—sharper, more insistent—cut through her thoughts.

Her stomach tightened. For a heartbeat, she thought it might be *his*.

"Who is it?" she called.

The voice that answered wasn't Jackson's. This voice, though muffled, was familiar and impossibly out of place.

Cautiously, she crossed the room and peered through the peephole. The sight of him made her pulse stutter. *Mitchell.*

Her hands shook as she slid the chain free.

"Mitchell? How did you—how did you know where to find me?"

"Conner told me," he said easily.

She blinked. "He didn't say—"

"I asked him not to," Mitchell said, and smiled—a small, regretful tilt of the mouth that was all too familiar. "Can we talk?"

She hesitated in the doorway. "I thought we were done talking."

"I'm sorry for how things ended," he said, stepping into the doorway. "Every day you didn't come home from work, or every time I sat waiting for you...I guess I never accounted for how much I'd miss you when I didn't see you at all."

The words stuck in her throat. When Mitchell left, this was exactly what she'd wanted to hear. She wanted him to apologize, to admit walking away was wrong. Now, with Jackson...around, it felt different.

"What happened?" she asked.

"Honestly? I met someone," he admitted. "She seemed like she could provide something that you weren't."

Her breath hitched as she processed his words. "I didn't give you what you needed, Mitchell, but I didn't do it on purpose."

"Yeah," he said, stepping inside and holding out his hand. "I know."

She took it, feeling the familiar warmth of his fingers. "I never meant to hurt you."

"We hurt each other," he admitted. "I didn't see how hard you were working—I was selfish."

"Why couldn't we have talked like this before?"

"We let it go too far."

A silence stretched between them, heavy with everything left unsaid.

"So, about this other woman..." she finally said. "I've been sort of seeing someone, too."

"Sort of?"

"We've been on a few dates. I spent Thanksgiving with him and some friends here."

"Do you have feelings for him?"

"We haven't shared as much as you and I have." She hesitated. "I knew I'd be going home, eventually."

"Can we agree we both made mistakes?" Mitchell exhaled, rubbing his jaw. "Put that aside and figure out if we still have something?"

Molly considered going back to her empty apartment in Seattle. His things were still there, untouched. She hadn't even made it a full day alone before fleeing to Texas. Going back like that—it didn't feel right.

"I think so," she whispered.

"Good," Mitchell said with a grin. "How about dinner? I'm starving."

She nodded. "Sure. I just need a minute...to get ready."

Molly called Ana to cancel their nightly meeting.

"He what?" Ana practically shouted.

"Just showed up at my door."

"What about Jackson?"

"I don't know, Ana. I'm not staying, remember?"

"Be careful, Molly. This was already likely to hurt someone, now it's nearly guaranteed."

"I don't know...things are finally cleared up."

"What about Jackson? He won't like this."

"There's a lot of things he's done, I don't like."

"So, you're taking swings, now?"

"No..." she said, as she braced her arm against the bathroom counter and looked herself in the eyes. "I'm just trying to do what makes the most sense."

"That might be the stupidest thing you've ever said...sense? Neither you or Jackson are thinking straight here."

When Molly said goodbye to Ana, and stepped out of the bathroom, Mitchell was waiting for her. He was facing the mirror over the dresser and adjusting his tie into a perfect Windsor knot.

"You want to touch up anything before we go?" he asked,

gesturing in a circle at her boots, her sweater, and her loose curls.

"Oh," she said, glancing at her reflection. "I guess I could change."

Ten minutes later, she stepped out of the Calypso in heels, and her hair neatly pulled into a bun. The strands tugged at her scalp, and felt unnatural after weeks of wearing her hair loose. When the wind lifted the hem of her skirt, she pressed it down and longed for her comfy blue jeans.

"So, where were you thinking of going?" she asked.

"There's a well-reviewed steakhouse downtown."

A Rare Affair. It was exactly the sort of extravagant, pristine place Mitchell loved.

When their cab arrived, Mitchell had settled into the backseat as if nothing had changed between them. He moved first, and she went along.

No.

"Hold on, Mitchell," she said. "I have another place I like. Do you mind?"

He blinked. "Well, I guess not."

"Wonderful." Molly gave the cab driver Ms. Sally's address.

Mitchell listened as she filled the ride with details about what she'd grown to love about Serenity—the ficus trees, the Texas hill country, the banter at Patty Cakes Café. He didn't seem interested in her stories about fire ants or tamale trucks, but he was warm and attentive.

When they pulled up outside Ms. Sally's BBQ, he barely

masked his disappointment. His polished manners, however, kept him from saying anything. He'd held the cab door open and let his hand to rest on her back. He was *polite*.

Molly took his hand and pulled him inside. "I know it doesn't look like much, but trust me."

"Well—"

"Molly!" Ms. Sally bustled forward, beaming. "I was hoping to see you again. Same thing as last time?"

"Absolutely. And some fried pickles, too, please."

Ms. Sally grinned. "Coming right up."

Molly led Mitchell to a window seat overlooking the lake. It overlooked the spot where she and Jackson had once stood under the moonlight. Now, the water reflected the Texas sunset, hues of orange and pink stretching across the sky.

"The view is...pleasant," Mitchell remarked, then gestured vaguely to the rustic décor. "Seems a little out of place, though."

"It's part of the charm, and has the best food you'll ever taste."

"It doesn't look like it would earn a Michlin Star."

"Some people make good food, but they aren't looking for a star." Molly glanced around, taking in the worn wood floors and the smiling customers. "The food tastes like home here."

Ms. Sally arrived with their plates. "That's what I like to hear. Can I get you two something to drink?"

"Sweet tea and a couple of glasses of water?"

"You got it."

Mitchell ate slowly, picking at his food, making small talk.

Molly finally asked, "Well? What do you think?"

He hesitated. "Really? I'm surprised you like this. The barbecue is fatty, the coleslaw has too much mayo, and who in their right mind would fry a pickle?"

Her stomach tightened.

"I'm sorry," she said. "I thought you'd like it."

"Don't get me wrong," he said, dabbing his mouth with a napkin. "It's fine. Maybe next time we go to that steakhouse?"

She barely touched her food after that.

When Ms. Sally returned, she frowned. "Was everything okay, honey? Last time, you practically inhaled the food."

"It was wonderful, Ms. Sally. I guess I wasn't as hungry as I thought."

Ms. Sally squinted at Mitchell, unimpressed. "Well, you're always welcome here, hungry or not."

As they stepped outside, Ms. Sally gave Molly a quick hug, leaning in to whisper, "Next time, bring Jackson. That boy would make any girl hungry."

Molly tightened her lips to keep from smiling.

"So," Mitchell said, resting a hand on the small of her back. "Want to head back to your room?"

She stepped aside. "That's a little soon, don't you think?"

"I wasn't sure if I should get a room," Mitchell said, standing awkwardly, brows drawn together. Molly felt like his frustration was her fault. Like she wasn't behaving the way he expected. "Let's head back to my hotel," she said, her voice too smooth, too polite. "We'll get you checked in."

At the front desk, Mitchell tapped his fingertips along the composite marble counter, ignoring the cheerful fake daisies in a plastic flower box and the scuffed travertine tiles beneath his feet.

"There's a king suite available," the clerk said with a smile.

Mitchell nodded, civil but distant, his shoulders heavy with something unsaid. "Yeah, sure."

Molly didn't comment. She offered a quiet "Thanks," her voice dipped softer, apologetic as her fingers brushed the rounded edge of the counter. She stepped away, glancing back once with a smile that didn't quite reach her eyes.

As they walked to the elevator, his footsteps lagged behind hers, unhurried, reluctant. Inside the elevator, she leaned against the corner, arms folded, watching the floor numbers blink upward while Mitchell stole quick glances at her. Neither spoke.

Back in her suite, Molly walked straight to the window where Mitchell's sleek luggage waited.

"There you go," she said, too bright, gesturing toward the bag. "Right where you left it."

He didn't move. His gaze traveled around the room, and then back to her. He stood near the door like he was searching for a reason to stay.

She felt it immediately.

The atmosphere shifted. It was familiar, but uneasy, like muscle memory gone stale. She turned, not meeting his eyes, and drifted toward the bed where her open portfolio spread beneath the circle of a warm-lit lamp.

"I've been organizing some of the Calypso details," she said, her tone casual, controlled. "Still a thousand things to finalize before the unveiling."

Fingers brushed the glossy documents—renderings, notes, line items—clean and sharp, like the image she'd built of this project, of herself.

He stayed quiet, but she heard the slight rustle behind her as he stepped in closer.

"I started mapping out the guest experience timeline," she continued, lifting a print. "The main lobby will have transitional lighting, sensor-triggered art installations, fragrance shifts tied to the time of day...subtle, immersive cues." She glanced back. "I want people to feel transported."

Mitchell nodded, but his eyes weren't on the plans.

"They'll love it," he said, but the compliment felt muted, empty around the edges.

"So what do you think?" she asked aloud, flipping the top page over, though he no longer stood behind her. "This is the Calypso. A custom-carved banister in the restaurant. Indoor herb wall. Vintage sconces in the ballroom next to a high-gloss mirrored ceiling..."

She trailed off.

He hadn't really been listening when he stood there, palms on her shoulders. Not when he brushed his fingers beneath the hem of her shirt or pressed a practiced hand to her bare thigh.

She'd flinched, not obstinately, but instinctively. It was too familiar. Too rehearsed. She realized it was a part of her past, and it no longer seemed to fit.

"I was thinking maybe I don't need that room tonight," he'd murmured against her jaw, lips skimming familiar paths.

Three years ago, that voice would've undone her.

Tonight, it made her ache in a different way.

His kiss—warm, familiar, textbook—elicited nothing. No flutter. No heat. Instead, she felt...distracted. Guilty, even.

Her hand grazed the back of his neck—out of habit, not hunger—and she knew she couldn't fake it anymore.

"Mitchell. Stop." She eased back, lowering her gaze to the carpet and speaking gently. "I'm sorry. It's just...It's too fast."

He blinked, fingers still hovering near her waist. "Fast?" The chuckle that followed was faint, disbelieving. "We hit a home run the first night we met."

"I remember," she said, folding her arms.

"So?"

"You're right. Maybe we need to do things a little differently this time. This means a lot to me. You came down here. I want to make sure that we don't screw it up, again."

Behind her, Mitchell shifted. "You've changed."

The words weren't cruel, but they sliced clean. Not judgment. No praise. Just observation.

She nodded. "I needed to."

At some point, she realized he'd moved to his suitcase. His fingers curled around the handle.

Then his gaze returned to her. "Yeah, I get that. Let me know when you're awake in the morning? Maybe we can go out to breakfast and you can take me to see your little hotel project."

"We didn't get it right last time," she said. "I want something better now. I think we both do."

The edges of her old life weren't lining up. Could she get it back? She didn't know, but she did know that when Jackson touched her, her world tipped sideways. Right now, Mitchell wasn't making her feel like that.

Instead she said, "Sure, I'd like that." Her head nodded yes, but her heart wondered if that was a good idea. She led him to the door, standing still while he leaned in for a goodnight kiss.

"I missed you, Molly"

She couldn't quite bring herself to say the words he wanted to hear. Instead, she pasted on a smile and said, "Goodnight, Mitchell."

And when the door finally clicked shut, Molly curled onto the bed, legs tucked beneath her. Mitchell had once been all she wanted: dependable, driven, safe, and..home in Seattle.

But Jackson?

Jackson was tool belts, and BBQ, and something she didn't even know she needed.

With a sobering clarity, she realized Mitchell had fit perfectly once, but now? He didn't feel quite right.

Chapter Twenty-Seven

Jackson

"Who is that guy?"

Jackson's voice came out low, a slow grumble under his breath as he squinted toward the figure walking along the curved path by the hotel. The summer sun burned bright, but the heat prickling at the back of his neck had nothing to do with the Texas weather.

It wasn't anger that tightened his shoulders.

It was instinct. Awareness. The same reflex he had on every job site when something unexpected stepped into a space he was responsible for.

Molly stood beside him near the pool, all golden curls and tight lines, her stance casual—but Jackson wasn't buying it. Her shrug seemed too practiced, as if she was bracing for impact.

"Mitchell," she said. "My ex-boyfriend."

Jackson raised one brow beneath the brim of his cap, tugging it lower with a callused thumb. "He doesn't seem very ex," he said, voice tighter than intended.

Not because he wanted to control the situation.

Because he didn't like being blindsided where Molly was concerned.

She shot him a sidelong glance. "Like you're one to judge. I have one word…Jessica."

His jaw tightened. "Low blow, Molly."

She turned to face the pool again, arms crossed. Calm. Controlled.

"We're talking about stuff," she offered.

"Talking, huh," he echoed, eyes drifting to the path where the guy—Mitchell—was clearly sizing up the hotel like it owed him something.

Jackson worked his jaw and shifted his stance, peeling his gaze from the sleek prick in slacks to focus on the landscaping—anything to stop Molly's shampoo from drifting across the three inches of air between them and muddling his thoughts.

Easy. This is her life. Not something for you to manage.

"What do you think of the layout?" he asked, gesturing toward the palm trees arching high near the glittering turquoise water.

She didn't miss a beat. "The palm trees by the pool are incredible. I never thought that swampy cesspool could turn into this perfect shade of jewel-toned blue."

He smirked.

"The guys did a good job making it look tropical. I wanted it to feel like a vacation spot for people who don't live near water."

"Well, mission accomplished. The kids are going to love

the little sandbox," she said. Her laugh was soft, but genuine. "Maintenance, not so much."

Jackson stepped forward then—wasn't a plan, just instinct—closing a bit of the space between him and Molly.

And just as quickly, he caught himself.

She didn't need him bracketing her. She wasn't fragile. She wasn't his to position.

"I may have skipped a few...relevant details," she said.

Oh, so that's how we're playing it? He narrowed his eyes slightly.

"So," Jackson said, voice low as he bent to retrieve another palm frond, lungs full of cedar mulch and Molly's perfume, "you didn't tell him we lived together?" A slower step now, deliberate as a measured pour. "That I know exactly where to touch you to make you groan?"

She froze, throat bobbing as she swallowed, eyes flicking toward him before darting toward Mitchell. "It was less than two weeks."

"But it was long enough for me to figure out just what makes you moan."

He had a beat—half a heartbeat—where smug satisfaction curled at the edges of his chest like smoke.

Then he shut it down.

That wasn't who he wanted to be. Not with her.

But it vanished when Mitchell's footsteps sounded behind her.

"Molly, there you are," the man said. "That older contractor said you'd be in the ballroom, but you weren't. Then he told me to check the kitchen."

Jackson leaned down to grab another stray palm frond and tossed it off to the side.

"What are you two talking about?"

The guy's voice made the hairs on his neck lift—collared polo, crisp khakis, and a polite expression that he didn't buy for a second. I'd bet a thousand dollars that guy has never callused a single little finger.

Molly glanced at Jackson, half-smiling. "Oh, just discussing sand."

He huffed out through his nose and adjusted his tool belt, hooks rasping against the leather like knuckles cracking. Not because he wanted to intimidate. Because he needed somewhere to put the tension.

"We also talked about you."

Mitchell cocked an eyebrow. "I doubt that."

Molly reached out and touched Mitchell's arm—light, familiar. It didn't sit well.

Not because she owed him anything. Because he hated the idea of anyone assuming they still had a claim on her.

"Sorry to make you wander,"

He shrugged. "Gave me a chance to look around. This must be the guy." He turned and held out a hand. "Mitchell Bishop. Nice to meet you."

Jackson stared at the offered hand for a moment too long. Then he took it.

Firm. Professional. Not a challenge. A boundary.

"Jackson Beaumont." He didn't miss the way Molly held her breath. "So, what do you think of the Calypso?"

Mitchell glanced around, nodding once, eyes indifferent.

"It's...different. I'll be interested to see what Paul and Maherson think. This is a big departure from their typical projects."

Jackson's jaw flexed. "I think it's going to change things for NorthStar," he said. His gaze swung back to Molly before flickering to Mitchell. "The vendors, local contractors—everyone's excited about it."

"I'm sure they are."

Jackson didn't move as Mitchell turned back to Molly.

"Ready to go?"

She hesitated.

He saw it.

Not uncertainty.Choice.

There was a tiny pause the moment her eyes found Jackson again, like she was grounding herself before stepping forward.

"Yeah, sure."

Jackson remained still, hands at his hips as she laced her fingers into Mitchell's and walked away.

He didn't follow.Didn't call out.Didn't try to redirect her.

Because whatever she chose to do next had to be hers.

Chapter Twenty-Eight

Molly

Four days. That was how long she had until Paul and Mr. Ma-herson arrived in Texas. Molly threw herself into any distractions she could find. There were last-minute details, changes to the entertainment, dates with Mitchell. Anything to keep her from pacing her hotel room and worrying about what came next.

She was confirming the centerpiece delivery when her phone rang. Ana.

"You answered too fast. Tell me you're not still working."

"Of course I am. What else would I be doing? Three hundred people. Black tie. No room for errors."

"It's going to be *perfect*. You've planned for everything. I think you need a distraction." A pause. "Jackson suggested I call you."

Surprised, Molly sat up a little straighter. "I haven't heard from him in days. How's he doing?"

"The guys say he's overworking them, but considering he's

already planned their Christmas bonuses, I think they'll survive."

Molly asked, "So, what does he need?"

"The Community Center's Christmas Festival is tonight. He thought you'd like to come. Everyone misses you."

She glanced at Mitchell sprawled across the couch, his laptop balanced on his legs. "Well, I'd need to bring Mitchell."

Ana made a dismissive sound. "Or...you don't."

"He's flying back soon. Seems rude to abandon him."

"He's a grown man."

"I'll ask if he wants to come. I'll text you in a minute." Ana huffed. "Fine."

Molly hung up. "Honey?"

Mitchell didn't look up right away. "Yeah?"

"What do you think about going to a show tonight?"

Tilting his head, he assessed her. "What kind of show?"

"Something local. A friend invited me."

He grimaced. "Tonight? I was hoping for a quiet night in."

"It's low-key." She tried to keep her tone light. "I could go alone."

Mitchell rubbed his temples with a sigh. "No, you don't need to go alone. Let me finish up here, and I'll get ready."

A little over an hour later, Molly navigated her rental car down old streets, past twinkling Christmas lights, and decorated shop windows. There were holiday lights curled around telephone poles like candy canes, and a local band's not-quite-tuned rendition of "Jingle Bell Rock" played from someone's open garage.

Mitchell's frown deepened the farther they drove. "This part of town feels...off."

She passed houses lined with warm lights and plastic Santas. "It's old. And charming," she said, voice clipped.

When they pulled into the parking lot, Mitchell stared at the brick building with a dubious arch of brow. "Is this a school?"

"It used to be. Now, it's the Community Learning Center."

"So...we're here for an amateur play?"

She cringed, then flashed a guilty smile. "More like a holiday sing-along?"

His expression was flat.

Before he could answer, she spotted Richie wheeling toward the entrance. "Hey, Richie! Merry Christmas!"

His face lit up. "Ms. Molly! You came to hear us sing?"

"Of course! I couldn't miss it."

Inside, Ana greeted them with a knowing smirk. Jackson stood to the side—quiet, tall, in a navy button-down that did unspeakable things to her pulse. His sharp blue eyes flickered between her and Mitchell.

"I wasn't expecting you," he said, adjusting his stance.

Molly turned to Ana, raising her brows in question before looking back at him. "I really wanted to see the kids perform."

Jackson's gaze softened. "It's going to be great."

They walked into the gymnasium, weaving past tables of cocoa and cookies, paper chains, and wreaths made from glittering green hand prints. Christmas lights brightened a dark hallway leading into the cafeteria, where the celebration was in full swing. A wreath made of pasta noodles hung somewhat askew near the stage. She couldn't help but love every inch.

Molly took it all in, heart swelling. "Jackson, this is incredible. You made *this* possible."

He rubbed the back of his neck. "It needed to be done."

Ana grinned. "He likes to play the hero."

A mother nearby pulled Jackson into a hug. "You are a hero."

His cheeks flushed red as he hugged her back. "Just doing my job."

Molly laughed softly, reaching out to squeeze his arm in teasing reassurance. His eyes darted to hers again, and for a breath—just one—they stayed there.

She touched his arm, shifting closer. "How are you holding up?"

He hesitated, and said, "Not sleeping much."

"Too much on your mind?"

"You could say that."

She lowered her voice. "Ana said you invited me, but you seem surprised I'm here."

"Ana makes trouble for fun."

Her stomach twisted as Mitchell came back with cocoa and cookies.

On stage, an older woman tapped the mic and said, "Hello? Thank you all for coming!"

Mitchell nudged her. "We should sit."

Molly hesitated, glancing back at Jackson. "It was good to see you."

His slight nod was all the response she got before she followed Mitchell to their seats.

From across the room, Jackson took his own seat near Ana, close to the stage. His gentle smile made her stomach flip.

A hush rippled through the crowd as the lights dimmed. On stage, children filed out, faces blooming with both nerves and candy-induced energy. A pause. A shaky microphone check, and then, from the smallest among them, came the first note of *Silent Night*. The spirit of the season, the belonging, the *rightness* of being here—Molly closed her eyes, and let the music wash over her.

Her throat tightened. She turned her head just slightly. Jackson sat in profile, expression neutral but soft. His hand lifted quietly to wave at a boy on stage, who grinned and waved back with both arms.

Something inside her pulled. Not tight or hard. Just gently toward him. And in that moment, she didn't want to be seated next to Mitchell.

She wanted to be next to Jackson.

Chapter Twenty-Nine

Molly

"An hour, I only have an hour!" she said, then started rifling through her clothes again. "I want them to know how seriously I take this."

Molly frantically pulled clothes from her dresser, pacing in front of the mirror as she modeled each outfit. After each wardrobe change, doubt crept in, and she'd shake her head before shoving the discarded option back into a drawer, or the closet.

Mitchell approached, wrapping an arm around her waist and pulling her close. "Molly, you've done everything you can to prepare. The color of your blazer won't change anything." He lifted her chin with a fingertip, meeting her gaze before pressing a small kiss to the tip of her nose. "Pick something. Anything. We'll grab lunch, then you can take me to the airport this afternoon."

She wiggled free, frustration flaring. "This has to be a win, Mitchell."

"It will be."

"I don't know how you can be so calm. This is the biggest day of my life."

"If it doesn't work out, we'll figure something else out." He turned to the mirror, adjusting his tie as he spoke. "You've got options."

She folded her arms, staring at his reflection. "This isn't a hobby."

"Of course not." His tone was breezy, almost dismissive. "But I've watched you chase this for years. It's just been one hoop after another. I guess I don't think it'd be the end of the world if you didn't get the promotion."

Fire flared in her chest. "Excuse me? You don't think I deserve it?"

"I want you to have whatever you want. I just don't think it's the only thing that matters," he said with a shrug. "We'll want kids, right? It only makes sense that you'll want to be home with them, too. Even if you get this promotion, it's not forever."

Her breath caught. "You need to leave. I can't do this right now."

He exhaled sharply, throwing his hands up. "Remember what your job has done to *us*," he said as he strode to the door. "I'll head to my room and you can have some...space." The quiet settled back into the room—the temporary calm before the day caught up with her.

Molly stood frozen in the silent room, fists clenched, jaw tight. Then, with a frustrated huff, she threw the shirt she'd been holding at the closed door. She turned and surveyed the hotel room. It was missing the Calypso amenities, but it had felt like a safe place. She'd spent more than work hours here. She'd missed Halloween, cobbled together her last-minute Thanksgiving with Jackson's friends, and even helped plan a community Christmas event she wouldn't be around to celebrate. The recent months in Serenity, Texas, felt fuller than a year back in Seattle.

Sure, she had Mitchell. She had Mama Malone's. She'd have the job she'd fought so hard to keep. But here...here, she had *more*.

There were children at the community center, her friendship with Ana, and, though she couldn't quite let herself put a label on it, there was Jackson. The thought made her chest ache. Perhaps she wasn't ready for a family, but she *was* ready to be part of something bigger.

"You're going home in a few days, Molly," she said to herself.

Restless, she gave up on picking an outfit and started sorting her belongings instead. "How did I end up with all this stuff?" She folded and stacked clothes into neat piles.

Her wardrobe had doubled. The polished pencil skirts, tailored suits, and sky-high heels she'd brought from Seattle sat neatly folded beside the jeans and cowboy boots she'd accumulated here. Two very different versions of herself were laid out before her—past and present.

Molly grabbed her phone and called the front desk. "Can you send up a few boxes?"

Now, she'd have to stop at the post office on top of sending Mitchell off. With renewed purpose, she folded her jeans and T-shirts, placed her boots on top, and packing away the last of the paperwork from the Calypso.

"Two boxes," she said, and patted the cardboard. "Just like that, my life tidied up." Before she could dwell on the thought, her phone buzzed.

"Hello?"

"Hey," Jackson's voice rumbled through the line. "You ready?"

She swallowed. "I'm scared."

"You've put a lot into this."

"Thanks for not telling me it's all going to be fine."

She could *hear* his smile when he said, "I've already told you. I see you, Molly. And I know you want more than *this*."

Her fingers tightened around the phone. "Where are you?"

"Leaving the house," he said. "Heading to the Calypso. Thought I'd see if you wanted to meet me there."

Her eyes flicked to the door as her thoughts flashed to Mitchell. After his pacing had made her dizzy, she was glad that they'd planned for him to leave later today. She needed to do this...*without him*, but maybe she didn't need to do it *alone*.

"Yeah," she said, exhaling. "I'm grabbing what I'll need for the day. Give me thirty minutes. I'll meet you in the lobby."

In the lobby of the finished Calypso, Molly watched the hustle and bustle around her. She'd spent the last two weeks moving furniture, monitoring the installation of equipment, and training staff.

NorthStar Investments had arranged transfers for some

employees to come from other properties they managed and owned. The rest of the hotel's employees were locals. The staff wore crisp uniforms in tailored black that stood out from the white walls and colored art. They looked like posh models at an art exhibit. Molly loved it.

Everything about the new Calypso was perfect. The glass and chrome sparkled, the art popped, and the staff appeared competent and ready for the guests arriving later that day. "Breathe," Jackson whispered in her ear.

Her squeak echoed in the ceilings high lobby and a few employees stopped to stare. Turning to face him, she admonished, "Don't do that!"

Jackson laughed, and said, "But it's fun trying to guess how high you'll jump." His gaze shifted from the door back to her. "Still waiting for the big guy, huh?"

"The flight confirmation said that the plane has landed. I don't know if they're stopping for anything, or coming straight here."

"Have you called them?"

"No, I don't want to come off too excited."

Another laugh rumbled out of him. "So, you're going for worried sick instead?"

"I'm going for confident, prepared, and capable."

"You have two of those down for sure."

"Thanks," she said with an eye roll and a tilt of her head. "I must be distracted. How could I have missed the suit?"

Jackson's wore a tailored navy pinstripe suit, white button-up shirt, and a dark navy tie with paisley flowers in violet. The polish on his shoes left them with a high shine. "I'm not throwing around hammers today, so I thought I'd dress for the occasion."

"I like the tie," she said as she rubbed her hand down the paisley fabric.

He caught her hand against his chest. "You're alone today."

"Yeah."

He tilted his head to the side. "You two still talking?"

"Yeah."

"Let me know if you stop."

He was different. It couldn't just be the suit? Could swapping a tool belt for a tie really change so much? She wondered what else she'd failed to see. The concierge tapped her shoulder before she grew too introspective.

"Ms. Monroe?"

"Yes, Becky?"

"I got a phone call from Paul and Mr. Maherson. They wanted you to know they're in the car you sent, and they'll be here soon."

"Well, that was thoughtful of them." She turned, gave a nod to Jackson, and then headed towards the receptionist's desk. "Let's make sure we have everything ready."

After confirming the rooms for Paul and her boss, she wandered to the kitchen to ensure the staff was ready to serve meals in the restaurant.

Details kept piling up, from VIP room checks to making sure housekeeping had the toiletries distributed properly. The pool was ready, and Molly confirmed that the parking crew had enough valet drivers, and they were ready to greet new arrivals.

When a long, black limo pulled up, she crossed her hands behind her back and squeezed her fingers tightly. Paul stepped out of the car, glancing at the Calypso, then at her. "So, you got it done, huh?"

"I told you I would."

Right behind him, Mr. Maherson climbed out of the vehicle. "Good evening, Ms. Monroe. I'm glad to see you're doing better than the last time we were here."

"I'm fully mended, thank you. How was your flight?"

"Not too bad. I'm looking forward to seeing what you've done here." The old man surveyed the scene: lush greenery, a path to the pool area, an almost empty parking lot, and the glass entryway to the Calypso. "So far it's looking good, Ms. Monroe. A vast improvement on the construction site we visited not too long ago."

"Mr. Beaumont has been a wonderful partner. There were a few close calls, but we've pulled through. Let me show you inside." She walked through the glass doors, holding her breath, then turned to watch Mr. Maherson's reaction. Her smile froze when she saw the look in his eyes. His frown made her blood run cold and her shoulders clench tight. "Is everything okay?" she asked.

"I don't think so, Ms. Monroe. What is going on here?"

"What do you mean?"

"This looks nothing like the design plans we discussed. This looks more like a Vegas casino than the high-end hotel establishment we had planned."

"I'm sorry. Paul said that he had discussed the changes with you." Molly looked accusingly at Paul.

He turned to their boss and, with an emotionless face, said, "Mr. Maherson, I'm not sure what she's talking about. We haven't discussed changes."

"Lies!" Molly realized that her voice was rising in volume. To avoid attracting attention from the staff, she took paused and attempted to speak to him a second time. "Paul, we talked about this. We've been discussing it for weeks."

Mr. Maherson turned to Paul and asked, "Is what she's saying true? Did you know about this?"

"We talked about making minor changes, things that stayed with in the design and structure. This is nothing like what we discussed."

Molly was feeling lightheaded. Mr. Maherson turned to her. "Why would you suggest Paul would make these changes without my permission?"

"He said we had your permission." Hurt shone in her eyes when she looked from Paul to her boss.

"Ms. Monroe, I'm rather disturbed and upset by this. I think I need some time to reflect. I would like to discuss this later. In the meantime, I'm going to speak to Mr. Beaumont and Mr. Taylor and decide how to proceed with this."

Like a punished child, she gazed at her feet and took a deep breath. She looked up, made eye contact with Mr. Maherson, and said, "Yes, sir. I can wait. Please understand that I made these changes with the best intentions. I really believe that this hotel is special, and this is in the best interest of the company. I can explain."

"And you will, but not this minute."

"Okay. Thank you." Molly stood rigid while Mr. Maherson and Paul walked to the receptionist's desk to check into their rooms. She watched Paul glance over his shoulder and give her a smug smile. She needed distance—not from the work, but from the moment—before everything demanded her attention again.

Chapter Thirty

Molly

"He did what?"

Molly stood near the window of the hotel room, city noise bleeding through the glass as Mitchell paced behind her. "He denied he knew anything about the project!"

"What do you mean by denied?"

"Paul said that we haven't been speaking, and that I never told him that we were making changes. He basically said I acted on my own free will."

The words landed hard.Not because Paul had disagreed with her—but because he had erased her judgment entirely.

"Don't you have records showing that you've sent him information?"

"I have emails I sent to Conner. Most of our conversations were over the phone. He said that Mr. Maherson trusted my judgment and I should proceed as I saw fit."

Trusted my judgment.That was what Paul had given her—until it became inconvenient.

"Molly, this is business. You know you should always have a paper trail."

"I didn't know I needed to protect myself against my coworkers, Mitchell."

Against people she'd built her career alongside. Against a system she believed rewarded competence.

"Now you're getting upset with me."

"You should back me on this."

He sighed. "Of course, I feel bad about your circumstances, Molly."

"I didn't say feel bad for me." Her voice sharpened despite her effort to keep it steady. "I need help figuring out how to fix this."

"Maybe you don't need to fix it. I still think that this whole promotion is a terrible decision. Maybe this is a sign. Maybe you don't want to work with these guys, anyhow. Plus, what happens if you get the promotion? You're still going to have to work with Paul, just as his manager."

"This is about more than the promotion," she said, heat rising behind her eyes. "This is about my honor. Mr. Maherson knows everyone. If he thinks I lied to him, it doesn't stop here. It follows me—to every firm, every boardroom, every recommendation I'll ever need."

She didn't need Mitchell to understand ambition.She needed him to understand consequences.

"I don't like the help that you're giving. I just found out that my coworker has been lying to my boss for the last three months. How am I supposed to feel? Relieved?"

"I don't need you to be snippy with me."

Molly stepped back, raising her hands. "You're right, Mitchell. I'm sorry that I am overreacting." The apology felt hollow even as she said it. "Unfortunately, with this change in this situation, I don't think I will be prepared to take you to the airport. Thank you for coming down here. I think it was very sweet of you, but you're going to have to see yourself home."

"Molly, that sounds like a cool goodbye."

"I would hate to have any actual emotion that you might think is inappropriately placed."

He took one step toward her. She took one step back.

"You obviously need some time to process this."

"Yeah," she said flatly. "You think?"

"I'm going to leave you alone and let you figure it out. We can discuss the next steps when you come back home. You'll be back tomorrow, right?"

"That was the plan." Her throat tightened. "After today, I'm not sure what's left for me here. But now I don't know if I'll have anything to head home to."

She saw his jaw set. She didn't want to hear whatever came next.

"We'll talk later, Mitchell."

He nodded once. "I'll call you when I'm home."

After she gave him a small nod, he left the hotel room.

When the door softly closed, Molly dropped to her knees and held her head in her hands.

The moments ticked by while she waited to find out what would be left standing.

"What the hell happened?" Ana said.

"I don't know," Molly answered. "Well, I know Paul and Conner are lying asses." She slammed her hand on the steering wheel and honked at the car in front of her.

"Are you driving?" Ana asked.

"Yes. I'm on my way back to the Calypso. I stepped away to deal with Mitchell, and now Mr. Maherson's secretary has ordered me back. I'm being summoned to my fate."

"Maybe he's busy with the event stuff this evening. I'm sure he didn't mean to be rude."

"Ana, we have done so much to make this happen. Our lives have stopped for months. The Calypso is gorgeous. It's a work of art." Her grip tightened on the wheel. "But he's not even going to see that. He's going to think I was some maverick who went on a rampage without permission."

Every measured decision.Every careful calculation.Reduced to recklessness by someone else's lie.

"Have you heard from Jackson? I know he was there today."

"Yeah. I saw him at the Calypso before they arrived. I had to leave before he ran into the two of them."

"Jackson will back you."

"Even if he does, he only knows what I told him. Mr. Maherson will think I lied to him, too."

A car horn blared beside her.

"You need to hang up," Ana said firmly. "I don't want you in a wreck on top of this."

"Sure," Molly said, her voice flat.

After the third car honked, she regretted driving. A cab would've been smarter. Stupid rental car. She'd been doing fine letting people give her rides—until Mitchell showed up and made it feel like something she shouldn't need.

What was I thinking?

It hadn't seemed necessary to go beyond Paul for permission. Maherson delegated. *Trusted.* Or at least she thought he did.

Her thoughts spiraled, tightening around her chest. "So stupid and naïve," she muttered, smacking the steering wheel again.

By the time she pulled up to the Calypso, she was flushed and nauseous.

"Don't give those back to me," she said, handing the keys to the valet.

"Yes, ma'am," he stammered.

"Please have someone take the rest of my bags up to my room. Betty will know where I'm staying."

"And your name?"

She didn't stop walking. "Ms. Molly Monroe. I'm the manager here." Then, quieter: "At least for right now."

Inside, Betty immediately began listing problems.

Molly paused, torn.

If she rushed Maherson, guests would suffer. If she delayed him, her job might.

Honor wasn't just defending yourself. It was choosing responsibility anyway.

"He can wait," she muttered.

"Pardon me?"

She grabbed pen and paper. "Begin again."

Point by point, she organized solutions. Delegated. Fixed. When Betty mentioned the caterer and entertainer issues, Molly felt the ground shift—but she didn't freeze.

This was her work. This was her integrity in motion.

When she finally stood before Mr. Maherson, her instinct screamed to defend herself.

She didn't.

She listened.

As he spoke—of trust, of disappointment, of Paul's account—Molly understood the true cost.

This wasn't about approval. It was about whether her word still mattered.

"I was hoping for some resolution today," she said quietly.

"Unless you want that decision to be your job," he replied, "I suggest you give me time."

She nodded. She shook his hand.

As she turned to leave, one truth settled firmly in her chest:

No promotion was worth surrendering who she was.

Whatever happened next, Paul's lie would not define her career.

Chapter Thirty-One

Jackson

Jackson found her in the kitchen—storming, pointing, and moving like a five-foot firework wrapped in business casual. She was in her element.

"Okay—listen up," Molly said, clapping her hands once to cut through the noise. "We're switching to contingency service mode. First, centerpieces on the tables, no glass refills until doors open. Second, confirm the new caterer's delivery window and reroute staff to the west prep station. Third, sound check the stage now, even without the entertainers. I want to know exactly what we're working with."

Staff scattered like startled pigeons, answering on the fly before darting from her path. It was impressive—like watching a general direct an army before battle—with a clipboard instead of a bayonet.

"And someone get me Betty," she added. "If the band's delayed more than thirty minutes, we move to Plan B. I don't want guests noticing a gap."

"You really should have avoided property development," Jackson said. "I think you missed your calling as an army general."

Molly turned when she heard his voice. She didn't smile, but glared at him with the exhaust-fueled fire of a woman clinging to the last tendrils of her composure. "You could have stopped at skipped property development and it would've been fine."

Heat flashed under her words. Not playful. Not flirty. Cutting enough to sting.

He scrubbed a hand down his jaw, watching her give a nod to a man holding a tray of tiny pastries before turning back to him. She looked like a lit fuse on dynamite.

"The meeting went that bad, huh?" he asked carefully.

"Yeah, he and I talked." Her voice stayed tight. Controlled.

"And?" Jackson asked. "I tried to assure him—"

"Thanks," she cut in, already turning back to the room, "but reassurance doesn't solve tonight's logistics."

She pointed again. "If the caterer's fridge failure pushes hot food past temp, we pivot to heavy hors d'oeuvres first, plated dinner second. Guests mingle, no one notices. If the band misses their slot, we bring in the kids' choir early and reset the schedule around them."

She finally looked at Jackson, eyes sharp. "I can't prove Paul lied. But I *can* make tonight flawless. And if tonight's flawless, maybe Mr. Maherson has no choice but to see the truth."

That's what this was about now. Not just a job. Not even the promotion. This was her line in the sand.

Jackson swallowed, the knot growing in his throat. He

wanted to ease some of her burden, but she wouldn't let him...not today.

Before he could respond, the chaos shifted again.

"Molly!" Ms. Sally's voice boomed like a Sunday football announcer, and she shuffled into the kitchen carrying a tall stack of boxes.. Behind her, Duncan stumbled in, arms overloaded with trays, his wide eyes peeping from behind a precarious pyramid of baked goods.

Jackson stepped forward on instinct. "Let me help."

He grabbed the top boxes from Duncan's stack, preventing him from face-planting into a warming tray. "Who decided you were the pack mule today?" he teased.

"You said, 'Do whatever I'm told.' So I did," Duncan grunted before slipping past him and setting the rest on the counter.

"Oh, thank you so much for being here," Molly said, her tone finally softening. She helped slide the trays onto the countertop with purpose, grace barely hiding panic.

Ms. Sally, pint-sized and iron-willed, yanked Molly into a warm squish of an embrace. "Hun, I'm glad you called. I already had the cooks going all afternoon for the dinner rush, now we'll be ready to go if we can get set up."

"I'm so sorry you can't be at the restaurant tonight."

"It's fine," Sally waved off the apology. "We simplified the menu, and pulled out some meat for burgers. No one's going hungry tonight—here or there."

Jackson stepped in beside them, glancing at Molly.

"You have her catering?"

"Our other one had their fridge die. I couldn't risk bringing in someone new. It may not be high-end cuisine, but the locals will love it."

He didn't have to fake the grin that broke across his face. "It'll be perfect," he said. "I think you just made her whole year."

Ms. Sally gave him a sly look and pinched his side hard enough to leave a mark later. "Careful now. You're just charming enough to weasel out of any cleanup if you keep talking like that."

"Yes, ma'am," Jackson answered like a man who knew better than to argue. "I'll keep the compliments to a minimum and focus on carrying things."

"Good boy."

Within minutes, the kitchen was transformed. Every surface was filled with platters of brisket and spiced cornbread, bowls of collard greens, and mini pies arranged in baskets tied with satiny ribbon.

It wasn't the bone-in lamb chops Molly had probably envisioned when she made the original plans, but hell—it smelled like love and would taste like comfort. He doubted any guest would complain once they tasted Ms. Sally's pecan pie.

As the kitchen buzzed with activity, Jackson found himself watching Molly, again. The lines around her eyes softened slightly. She looked less like she was bracing for earth-shattering impact, and more like a woman retraining herself to hope.

"I'm going to go check on the ballroom and entertainment," she said finally, giving Sally one last squeeze.

Jackson didn't stop her. He didn't ask what Mr. Maherson had said or beg her to take a ten-minute nap before she collapsed. This wasn't his moment.

It was hers.

All he could do was clear her path. And, if that meant she walked her right out of his life? Well, he'd still be glad he helped. And Jackson? He was just lucky to have stood beside her long enough to witness it.

Molly walked into the ballroom and let gasp. The interior decorators had transformed the ballroom into a winter wonderland.

There was an ice statue of a reindeer rearing up on its hind legs, the room was ringed in snow-flocked trees, and crystal beads hung beside shimmering white Christmas lights. The result was a Christmas disco.

Cream cloths covered the tables, and silver ribbons backed the chairs. The centerpieces were the chrome buckets Ana had monogrammed filled with spider plants, holly and acrylic, glitter dipped twigs that looked like they were forming icicles.

No less than six Christmas trees decorated the stage, which was fronted with fluffy clouds of white tulle and crystal lanterns glowing with light. The stage, however, was not occupied by musicians.

She grabbed a bus boy that was wandering by. "Have we heard from the entertainers, yet?"

"Ms. Betty said they're still running late."

With a sigh, she walked out of the ballroom. A small part of her hoped she would find the entertainers waiting in the lobby, but she knew wishing wouldn't make them show up. She hoped her B plan would work.

Molly looked around. For the first time in hours, there was no one calling her name, or asking her to fix something, "Ten minutes" she said to herself, and headed for the bay of elevators. Betty had been waiting with her key after the meeting with Mr. Maherson. She'd planned for more time to get ready, but her priority was preparing the hotel.

The plastic key slid into the door's lock and beeped. "Mitchell?" she said, when she pushed the door open to reveal a massive bouquet on the corner table across the room, filling the air with lilies and roses.

It didn't seem like his style. It was too extravagant. She brushed aside the fluffy greenery and spotted a card tucked between the stems. Carefully, she pulled the envelope out of the flowers and tore it open. Inside was a simple card.

You did this. I'm glad I could be a part of your team. Yours truly, Jackson <3

She held the card to her chest. It wasn't the first gift she had received from a contractor, or the first floral gift she'd received after a project. A small heart next to the sender's name, however, was new. She pulled her phone from her back pocket and sent him a quick text. *Thanks for the flowers.* Molly waited for a reply, but when silence followed, she placed the phone and card on the table and started to prepare for the party.

The gown she'd selected had hung in her hotel closet for weeks. She'd found it at Taylor's boutique and knew it would be perfect. The dress was a bold red satin with thin straps and a low-cut back. The fabric fell in layers down her back. Combined with a pair of dangling gold earrings and a waterfall of curls, she looked at her reflection in the mirror and smiled. With her makeup applied, her cheekbones were contoured, and her eyes were left smoky and mysterious.

A phone ding caught her attention and put a smile on her face. With hurried movements, she grabbed her clutch purse, slid on her heels, and rushed out the door.

When the elevator doors opened, Molly's smile stretched wide at the sight of the children and their parents filling the lobby. "You made it! Beth, thank you so much."

"That's what community is for." After wrapping Molly in a warm hug, Richie's mom stepped back and smiled. Molly lost count of how many hugs she'd had that day.

"And I'm so grateful for you! Grab everyone and follow me."

When the kids and their parents entered the ballroom, the already lively space filled with wows and excited chatter. Parents bent down, whispering in children's ears, and one by one, they nodded, lining up on the stage. Dressed in their festive formal attire, they looked just as adorable as they had at the center.

The kitchen had prepared a small banquet in another room for the parents to enjoy dinner and holiday treats while their choir instructor led the kids in song.

Glancing at her watch, Molly felt relief wash over her. Plan B was working. Guests would begin arriving in less than twenty minutes. The ballroom remained beautifully arranged, entertainment was now in place, and she knew Betty had everything under control with the hotel staff. She stopped in the kitchen before going out to welcome the guests.

As she pushed open the swinging doors leading into the kitchen, Ms. Sally was the first person she heard "Jackson, son, put those ribs in the warmer! Duncan, check on the corn in the pots! Jenny, right? Watch those rolls—don't burn them!"

If anyone had missed their military calling, it was Ms. Sally. Duncan, Jackson, and anyone else who came near her were enlisted.

When Sally turned and spotted Molly standing at the kitchen entrance in her bright red dress, she put her hands on her hips and grinned. "Well, aren't you a sight? I swear, I've never seen anything prettier."

Molly's cheeks warmed, but she ignored it. Over Ms. Sally's shoulder, she noticed Jackson had stopped working. His gaze locked onto her with an intensity that had nothing to do with the food in front of him.

"Everything going okay in here?" she asked Ms. Sally, keeping her voice even.

"Sure is. You've got a good team here."

"Thank you. I'm proud of every one of them." She let her gaze sweep over the bustling kitchen. A young girl in a white apron pulled trays from the ovens, while two members of the kitchen crew stood elbow-deep in soapy water at the sinks. The chaos and teamwork brought a lump to Molly's throat. The weight of the evening—the nerves, the struggles, the uncertain future—caught up to her, and her voice cracked as she said, "I couldn't have done any of this without such wonderful people."

Without hesitation, Ms. Sally flicked a hand toward Jackson, and said, "Help her before she ruins all that fancy makeup."

"Yes, ma'am," Jackson said, crossing the room to her. His warm hand curled around hers. "Come on, let's find someplace quiet."

Chapter Thirty-Two

Jackson

He followed Molly out the side doors of the ballroom, the hush of the garden patio settling around them. The day's heat mellowed into a humid cloud, but the ground radiated heat, stubborn and unyielding. The Texas earth refused to let go. So did he.

"That dress is stunning on you," said Jackson.

Looking down, Molly smoothed the fabric between her fingers. "You wear a lot of hats, don't you?" She lifted a brow, glancing at his pinstripe suit—now covered by a flour-dusted white apron.

"I'm handy, and I like to be helpful."

Hell of a truth. He couldn't stand back while Molly's big night unraveled. Not after building so much with blistered hands, bruised pride, and sheer will.

"Cook, contractor, and construction tycoon," she teased.

He laughed low in his throat. That sound always rose easy around her. "I don't know about all that. You handle a fair number of jobs yourself." He angled his head, nodding toward the glittering glass doors behind them. "This entire event? That takes talent."

Her expression—guarded, almost too still—softened for the barest second.

"Thank you," she said, her voice drifting off.

That was the part that gutted him. She'd moved mountains and was still worried she hadn't done enough.

He glanced through the transparent wall of glass, spotting the chorus of kids jumping up and down, their burgundy sweater vests crooked, bow ties askew. A grin tugged at his mouth. "I see you figured out the entertainment situation. The kids'll talk about this night for years."

"It was the best I could think of on short notice."

"It was a brilliant plan." He turned back to her, chin tipping. "Are you ready for the guests to arrive?" What he really wanted to say was: *I'm not ready for this to be over. I don't want you to leave. Why can't you stay?*

"I think so," Her arms folded across her middle like she was holding herself together.

A quiet moment passed before he spoke again. "What happened back in the kitchen?"

Ah. The scene. Molly exhaled, one hand dragging across the back of her neck like she could wipe the tension clean off her skull.

"Life. Fate. A long friggin' day. Who knows?" she said, clearly not meaning to blurt out anything with witnesses, especially not while they were butter-basting pastries. "I know it wasn't professional. I'm sorry."

"You think you need to apologize to me for having feelings?"

She hesitated, her eyes finding his. "No. I seem to have a habit of apologizing for everything."

He gave a small snort. "Sounds like a bad habit." Jackson shifted, his hand twitching at his side, resisting the urge to tuck a piece of hair behind her ear—that golden curl that always slipped loose when she lost her cool and didn't want anyone to notice.

You're doing great. He wanted to say it out loud. Hell—he wanted to shout it until she actually heard him.

Instead, he looked out past her into the growing twilight, where quests would soon arrive and find wonder and awe...because she had made it so.

Something moved behind the glass. A couple in formal wear stepped through the front doors—tuxedo and sequins, all sparkle and expectation.

Jackson's chest squeezed. *Time's up.*

"Looks like the first guests are here," Molly said, smoothing her skirt. She turned to him, one hand curled on the door handle, the other trembling. "Thanks...wish me luck."

He was aching to reach for her. "With you? Luck's unnecessary."

She returned his smile, small and cautious. Then she stepped inside, back straight, shoulders squared.

Jackson stood there, watching the door slip shut behind her, already missing her. He wanted Molly Monroe to win, no matter what—more than his truck, his job, or his quiet life.

Even if winning meant she'd leave.

Chapter Thirty-Three

Molly

As soon as she stepped through the doors, the ballroom filled with the cheerful sound of children's voices singing *Deck the Halls*. The moment settled around her, bringing a tranquil ease to her heart.

"Welcome!" she said, greeting her first guests. "Hello, and welcome to the grand opening of the Calypso Hotel."

She positioned herself at the entrance, welcoming each new arrival. Everyone was excited, complimentary, and grateful to be part of the evening's festivities.

While she was talking to a couple about how the new hotel would help the town, Paul strolled past, his expression cool and detached, his glance dismissive.

Molly lost her train of thought, and ended up stammering an apology to the couple. "Pardon me. I need to check on something. Please enjoy your evening."

She turned away and moved instinctively in the opposite direction from Paul—only to nearly collide with Mr. Maherson.

"Good evening," he said. "How are things progressing?"

"Wonderfully, sir. The guests are mingling."

His eyes flicked toward the stage. "Are those children up there?"

"Yes," she said, trying to keep her breathing stable. "Our original entertainer ran into some technical difficulties, so the children are our opening act."

His lips curved. "And where did you find them?"

"I have my sources," she said, keeping her tone light.

"So, I see. It's a pleasant touch."

Near the lobby entrance, she spotted the actual band arriving. Relief flooded her. "Excuse me," she said, nodding toward them.

"Certainly."

Molly moved, intercepting the musicians and directing them toward the stage. Maneuvering twenty-plus children off the platform while positioning a full orchestra in a small space was like collecting cotton balls in a snowstorm.

By the time the kids returned to their parents—each clutching a cookie—the orchestra had started playing soft Christmas music while the guests found their seats. Mr. Maherson seemed prepared to deliver his welcome speech.

Molly took a quiet breath, standing in the back of the ballroom. She scanned the room, checking for potential problems. Everything was in place.

Then, movement outside the patio doors caught her attention.

Paul.

He was stepping outside out into the garden patio, and he wasn't alone. Another man followed him—a man in a familiar pinstriped suit.

Jackson.

Molly's stomach tightened.

"What could the two of them be up to?"

The ballroom doors muffled the sound of applause as Molly slipped into the shadows of the corridor, heels clicking softly against the marble. She turned toward the glass patio doors near the far corner, glimpsing Jackson and Paul disappearing outside. Her chest tightened—not a snap, but the slow pull of something tangled and fraying.

Maybe she could follow. Maybe she could—

"Ms. Monroe?"

The voice cut through her thoughts. She turned, guilt and instinct curling around her spine, to see a staff member clutching a coiled microphone cord in one hand.

"We have a problem with the AV crew." His brow furrowed, his tie slightly askew. "They're missing some connections for the sound system."

Of course they are.

She glanced once more toward the patio doors—but the figures were gone now, swallowed into the dark. She squared her shoulders.

"Let's see what we can find," she said, voice calm, fingers already flexing with the weight of a dozen responsibilities.

The next thirty minutes blurred as she went on a scavenger hunt through storage closets and utility rooms that smelled like lemon-scented cleaner. They hadn't wired the stage for speeches, only relying on the pure strength of a small orchestra and the adorably off-key choir. But Mr. Maherson needed a mic—of course he did—and Molly needed to deliver it.

Then a frantic text popped up from the kitchen.

Custard cup issue. Come fast.

While rushing into the kitchen, her skirt caught on a sharp edge and tore with a delicate rip that made her wince. She'd barely resolved the second course plating issue, before Betty found her with a sewing kit and sent her to the ladies' room to MacGyver herself back together with a prayer and the worst stitch job seen outside of a Girl Scout camp.

When she finally stepped back into the bloom of soft lights and clinking silverware, guests were settling back into their chairs. Mr. Maherson stood near the edge of the stage, halfway through his speech, gesturing toward a vaguely appreciative crowd. Molly scanned the gold-lit tables and spotted Jackson and Paul, both seated like nothing had gone spectacularly wrong behind the scenes.

She hesitated in the doorway.

This wasn't the moment she'd imagined. The one she'd earned with late-night emails, months away from home. Love sacrificed on the altar of ambition."Stop it, Molly," she said to herself. The sharp click of her heels took her towards the kitchen.

Inside, the air was warmer, quieter, and filled with the comfort of cinnamon and rosemary and something sugary she couldn't quite name. Ms. Sally didn't stop. Instead, she raised an eyebrow, while chopping herbs with the precision of someone whose brisket softened the toughest men.

"Back already?" Sally asked without looking up.

"I need a snack before I develop a plan to throttling someone."

Without missing a beat, Sally scooped a few pecan pie bites onto a plate and set it at a prep station tucked between towers of gleaming dishware and a vat of whipped cream. Molly slid onto the stool, letting herself breathe. One bite, and the caramel and spices coated her tongue with a tempting thought...the satisfaction she'd been searching for her whole life might be right in front of her.

Across the kitchen, Duncan and two of Sally's sous chefs stole forkfuls of uneaten potato salad, laughing quietly behind a stack of pans. Chocolate smudged the old man's white cuff—he didn't seem to care.

Molly smiled faintly and took a second bite.

These people. This town. Even without being asked, they'd shown up. They made space for her. Instead of telling her to give up, they'd asked her how they could help. They never pretended her ambition was too loud or inconvenient—Jackson, least of all.

She should miss Mitchell. He'd always been steady, predictable. Her life had made sense to him. But instead of missing him, she just...remembered him.

And the satisfaction she thought tonight would bring? It wasn't missing. It was just...different. She didn't feel victorious. Just full.

Not with success, but with something quieter. Heavier. Something shaped like community and slow Texas mornings and navy-blue button-downs with sawdust on the sleeve.

She checked her watch—the full sweep of the minute-hand nudged her back to reality. She should be out there, watching Mr. Maherson delivering a speech, reclaiming her future, and rebuilding her dismantled reputation.

Sally's warm hand landed on her shoulder. "One last hug before you go?"

Molly slipped from the stool and wrapped her arms around her without hesitation—this woman with flour dust on her blouse and love for everyone she fed.

"Always, Ms. Sally."

The older woman gave her a lingering squeeze and whispered into her ear with a crooked grin, "We're about done here. Don't worry. We'll sneak out quick, and won't steal any of your leftover champagne."

"Security!" Pulling back, she found Sally's smiling eyes. "I'm sure they won't miss a few bottles...you deserve to celebrate, too."

Sally said, "You come by my place sometime. I'll feed you something that doesn't need to be served on fine china."

"I wouldn't miss it," Molly said, and she meant it.

With a last nod, Sally nudged her gently toward the door.

"Now get on out there."

So she did. Not triumphant, not perfect, but definitely not alone.

Chapter Thirty-Four

Jackson

Waiters scraped the plates. Laughter lingered in corners. The lights still burned low, soft and golden, dancing across the table linens that Molly had obsessed over for three weeks straight. She'd nailed it—every square inch of it was beautiful. Of course she had. That's who she was.

He'd had watched her all night. Watched her laugh and nod and smile so tightly it had to hurt. He saw her glance across the room watching for Paul, Mr. Maherson, the staff, the caterers—everything and everyone except him. He knew she'd felt the look he gave her from across the room, but he waited for her attention, because this wasn't his night. It was hers.

Jackson stood near the back of the room, just beyond view of the main hall. He'd long since loosened his tie, and had his hands curled into the pockets of his slacks. He didn't belong in a ballroom like this, with chrome lights twinkling like a diamond store and waiters in pressed jackets moving between the tables like ghosts. But, he was simply honored to stand here and watch her shine.

His gut was still twisting over the way she'd looked at Paul earlier. The betrayal. The disbelief. That bastard had lied through his teeth to save his own career and left Molly bleeding in front of her boss, careful to tuck the knife neatly between her ribs before walking off like he hadn't done a thing wrong.

Jackson was going to fix it. He lacked a business degree or a seat at a C-suite table, but he had something. Proof.

After Paul had stumbled off toward the ballroom earlier, Jackson had gone straight to the security desk and asked for the footage—every camera near the private entrance, every angle that might've caught a loose tongue and a careless drink.

He'd spent the night digging, and now it was time to show his cards.

He stepped out of the shadows, making his way around the last lingering guests. She was about ten feet away, brows pinched, scanning the room like she was missing someone important and couldn't quite pin down why.

He smiled gently. "Looking for someone?"

"Someone." She turned, surprised, but it was soft in the corners of her mouth. "Where were you headed?"

He took a steady breath, finally close enough to catch the warm citrus twist of her perfume. "Actually, I was lookin' for you." His voice dropped into something low, steady. "Do you think Maherson and Paul have a minute? There's something I'd like to show them."

She blinked, tension flickering across her face. Her eyes scanned his, reading something in them. Trust, maybe. Or a quiet desperation he wasn't doing a great job of hiding. "I think he'll be finished soon. The room's clearing fast. I hope people are excited to get back to their rooms."

He watched the retreating backs of the winded executives and buzzed investors. "Texans know how to make big exits."

She gave him a look—tired, but teasing. "I heard a rumor everything is bigger here." Her lips curved faintly upward, and it hit him deeper than it should've.

When the last few guests had trickled past, Molly stepped forward toward her boss. Jackson hung back, letting her make the approach.

"Excuse me, sir?" she said, voice even. "Is now a good time?"

Mr. Maherson turned, and Jackson stood taller instinctively. The man wore power like a suit.

"Ms. Monroe," he said. "You did a good job this evening." And that did it.

A flicker of pride tightened in Jackson's chest. God, he hoped that sat sweet in her bones for longer than half a second.

"Thank you, sir. I enjoyed your speech." Molly said, then stepped aside, motioning. "Jackson has something he'd like to speak with you about."

Mr. Maherson's eyes sharpened, turning toward him. "What can I do for you, Mr. Beaumont?"

Jackson cleared his throat, heart hammering. "If I could ask for a small amount of your time, I'd appreciate it. There's something I think you ought to see before the night's over."

He said, his eyes calculating.

Jackson continued, calm and sure. "If you wouldn't mind bringing Paul and Molly with you?"

A beat of silence, then Mr. Maherson turned toward the

concierge desk where his second in command was standing. "Paul? Let's go."

Paul's voice was level and clearly unconcerned despite the impromptu meeting. "Sure, sir. Lead the way."

As Jackson gestured toward the corridor leading to the staff offices, he caught Molly's eye.

She didn't say anything, but fell into step beside him.

The small security office was dim, cramped, and lit by the sterile flicker of outdated LED panels overhead. Jackson stood near the far wall, arms crossed. The air was thick with the lingering scent of burned coffee and static tension. He stared straight ahead, focusing on the bluish glow of the monitors, not on the woman next to him.

Molly stood a few feet to his right, silent, stiff, her arms knotted across her chest. She wasn't looking at him.

He could feel the tight coil of energy radiating off her. She was trying to hold it in, but he saw through it. If this ended with her leaving with a raise, a promotion, and a one-way ticket to Seattle—then he'd let her go. As long as she won, and this lie didn't steal from her what she'd worked her whole career to build.

Mr. Maherson sat in the lone chair like he ran the Pentagon, back ramrod straight, elbows bracing the arms of his seat, eyes flicking between screens as the security guard queued the playback files.

"Tonight, right?" the guard asked, tapping a few keys.

"Around 8:30 p.m.?"

"Yes, please," Jackson confirmed.

From the corner of his eye, he caught Molly's confused glance.

She didn't trust what was about to happen. Not fully.

He couldn't blame her for that either—not after the week she'd had.

The screen hissed to life, the lobby feed blinking once before fading into the exterior of the private ballroom entrance. For one breathless beat, it showed an empty patio—rustling palms under string lights and a pool of shadows beyond the stone terrace.

Then the door swung open.

The video captured Paul as he stumbled, drink sloshing in one hand, with a smug look plastered across his face.

Jackson saw Molly's lips part. Her brows furrowed slightly.

Then he appeared on camera, trailing Paul. The way he held his drink was casual. The way he leaned on the railing—intentional.

Jackson couldn't plan for what the video would catch, but he knew one thing—Paul had an ego. He couldn't keep his mouth shut when he thought he was winning. People like him underestimated guys like Jackson. They thought they weren't smart enough. That they were only good for laying tile and pounding hammers.

"Turn up the volume," Jackson instructed quietly.

The small speakers cracked alive. Paul's voice filled the room—slurred, but smug.

"Need another?"

Jackson's voice came through next. "Sure. I'm celebrating."

"Yeah. Molly really surprised me."

Even knowing what was coming, Jackson caught a flicker of movement beside him. Molly had gone still.

He wanted to reach over, clasp her hand, and tell her to wait. But not yet. His voice on the screen was smooth, designed to nudge, not confront.

"She's got a tendency to micromanage," his recorded self said. "But I never understood why she let Mitchell run all over her when she was such a nag at work."

Paul scoffed. "So, she pulls that with you too, huh?" Then he seemed to reconsider his words. "Honestly? It was nearly impossible working with her."

A sharp inhale came beside him.

Molly.

She turned to him, her profile pale under the flickering monitor light, eyes locked onto his like she'd just been sucker-punched mid-sentence.

He held up a hand.

Wait. Just wait.

"And yet, man," the recording of Jackson said, "you pulled this off."

A scoff from Paul. "Yeah—no thanks to her."

"Did she really handle all this on her own?"

"That's the thing...she didn't. I helped. I wasn't about to let our company take a hit. NorthStar Properties is my future, too."

Silence blanketed the room.

Then Jackson's voice returned in that same baiting calm.

"Then why'd you tell her boss you didn't know?"

"Eh. I wanted her gone," said Paul. "She's been after a partner spot for years. There's only room for one new partner at NorthStar. If she gets this promotion, it's her or me. If she's out of the way, it's mine."

That clipped, unapologetic truth hung heavy in the air.

But Paul wasn't done.

"I wasn't alone," he said. "Conner's been helping me for months. When Mitchell dumped her, I thought she'd spiral. Thought she'd crawl down here licking her wounds. Didn't expect her to fight back."

Bastard.

Jackson bit down on the inside of his cheek to keep from swearing out loud.

"...he 'forgot' to pass on meetings," Paul was still saying. "Sent her the wrong schedules! And the thing is, she never even figured it out."

Jackson's head shook on the screen as he asked, "So, you had her assistant working against her too? That's bold."

Paul's drunken pride practically oozed from the grainy security footage. "And it worked perfectly."

The last sound captured by the recording was Paul clapping Jackson on the back. Then the screen went black.

Silence dropped in its place, thick and deafening.

Jackson exhaled through his nose.

Beside him, Molly hadn't moved. But the tightness near her temples had eased—just barely.

Mr. Maherson turned in his chair. The swivel creaking like something from a courtroom drama. "What the hell is this?"

His voice was flat with quiet fury.

Paul blinked. "Sir, there's been a misunderstanding—"

"That," Maherson said, gesturing to the dark screen with controlled precision, "is not 'a misunderstanding.' That is sabotage."

Jackson watched Paul shift—shoulders taut, hands twitching.

Molly still hadn't said a word.

Finally, Mr. Maherson turned toward her.

His stony face softened, a flicker in his eyes when they landed on her. Regret. Embarrassment, maybe...for ever questioning her.

"I assume this means you've been telling the truth," he said.

"I tried—" her voice broke.

Jackson couldn't take it anymore.

"Obviously, he set her up." He stepped forward, edging closer to Paul. He didn't tower—he didn't need to, but he let the steel in his voice coat every syllable. "You heard it yourself," he said. "All of it. He used her. Undermined her. Spun every detail to suit his own goals."

Paul tried to fold his arms, couldn't. "Jackson," he started, false smile returning.

"No. Don't try to smooth this over. You toss your coworkers under the bus, that's on you. But Molly? She earned everything she's done here. And she would've taken that hit all alone if I hadn't caught this tonight."

He turned to Mr. Maherson. "Send him home. Let the company sort it out."

Maherson's expression didn't change, but his jaw ticked.

Turning toward Paul, his words were calm, but frosty. "Go back to your room. Now. You and I will have a conversation. If you're not interested in having it face-to-face, then I suggest you hop on the first flight out and start clearing your desk back home." His voice dropped dead quiet. "Because I swear to God, Paul...when I get back to Seattle, you won't step foot in my office ever again."

Paul hesitated—just barely—then nodded and walked out.

The room remained still until Maherson—slowly, carefully—stood up.

He turned back to Molly.

"I owe you an apology," he said. "You've shown honesty. Dedication. Loyalty. And resourcefulness under pressure—a lot of it. That is what I expect from my partners."

Her breath hitched.

Jackson knew what she was thinking.

Every sleepless night.

Every missed call from Mitchell.

One thousand questions about whether she was wasting her time.

This was the moment she'd been clawing her way toward her whole life.

"Thank you, sir," she said, fighting past the knot in her throat.

He adjusted his tie like he didn't know what to do with her gratitude. "We'll sit down and finish this officially when we're all back in Seattle. I need time to sort through a few changes internally." Then he looked at Jackson. "I owe you."

Jackson gave the man a firm handshake. "I don't like seeing

good people hurt by liars."

Mr. Maherson nodded once, then pointed a finger at Molly as he was walking towards the door. "See you Monday morning."

She nodded, dazed.

When the office finally emptied, Jackson turned to her and reached for her hand. Silent for a beat. Then softly, "You held every piece of this place together. Even when they tried to tear you down."

She looked at him, and the ache in his gut was too big for words. He let himself believe, for one long moment, that she might not leave.

Not just yet.

Maybe...

Maybe not ever.

Chapter Thirty-Five

Molly

While walking down the carpeted hallway of the Calypso Hotel, she slipped off her heels, sighing before stepping into the gleaming marble of the lobby. It was strange how familiar this place had become—a public space that felt almost personal.

"This lobby feels like my living room,"

"I don't know," Jackson said, his voice tinged with amusement. "I think I prefer the privacy of *my* living room."

"You know, I think I prefer the privacy of your living room, too." She shot him a sly glance. "Thank you...for being that guy."

He chuckled and said, "Figured it was worth a shot."

"What made you think of it?"

He tilted his chin upward, nodding toward a small security camera wired into the ceiling above them. "The Calypso just upgraded to state-of-the-art security. When you and I were on the patio earlier, I noticed the camera. Then I saw Paul down six cocktails and figured loose lips sink jobs." He shrugged. "So, I put the two together."

She exhaled sharply. "You saved my career, Jackson."

"I know how much it means to you. Even if it also means you're leaving."

"I couldn't have done this without you."

"Yeah, you could have. I just did the heavy lifting. You could've hired any lug for that."

She nudged him playfully. "Well, I'm glad the lug I ended up with was you."

Jackson reached into his blazer pocket, pulling out a small red box tied with a delicate, sparkling bow.

"But you already sent flowers!"

He placed the box in her hand. "Open it."

"But I didn't get you anything," she said.

"I don't need anything," he assured her. "I wanted to give you your Christmas present before you left."

She hesitated, glancing at the bustling lobby. "Here?"

He nodded.

The lid of the small box sprung open, and she inhaled sharply. Nestled against a cushion of red velvet lay a delicate silver necklace with a Texas-shaped pendant. A tiny diamond glittered near the panhandle—right about where Houston would be on a map.

She traced the edges of the charm with her fingertips, swallowing against the knot in her throat. "I love it."

"Good. I wanted you to remember what you found here."

He gently lifted the necklace and fastened it around her neck, his fingers brushing her neck in a way that sent warmth through her.

With one hand resting on the pendant, she pushed the elevator button. When the doors slid open, Jackson raised a questioning eyebrow.

"I have a few things I need to finish up tonight."

He gave a small nod, then stepped in closer, pressing a soft kiss against her cheek. His arm wrapped around her in a lingering embrace, his hand settling at the small of her back. He smelled of pine trees, cologne, and the dusty undertones of freshly cut wood. A scent that had become unmistakably his.

As she stepped into the elevator, she turned to him. "I'll check in before I leave tomorrow?"

"Will you?"

Before she could answer, the doors slid shut between them.

When the elevator arrived at her floor, she trudged to her room, the weight of the night pressing against her shoulders. She nudged open the door, tossed her heels into the closet, and collapsed onto the bed.

Her dress bunched around her hips as she rolled onto her back, staring at the ceiling. Frustration churned inside her. In one quick motion, she flailed against the mattress, smacking her hands and kicking her legs like an exasperated child. When she finally stilled, exhaustion settled in.

"What am I going to do?" she whispered to the quiet room.

Her thoughts spiraled—circling Jackson, then Mitchell, then wrapping around Paul before landing on Ana. Thoughts of cold, rainy Seattle bled into hazy Texas sunsets. The loneliness of her hotel room blurred into the squishy comfort of Jackson's couch.

When her phone rang, she fished it out of her clutch and answered without checking the display. "Hello?"

"How'd it go?"

"Mitchell—how was your flight?"

"It was fine. Weird coming back without you." His voice softened. "But you didn't answer...how did it go tonight?"

She hesitated. "I don't know, honestly. It was...just weird. Jackson saved my job."

"He did *what*?"

"Yeah, he pulled some crazy spy move and got Paul to confess to lying."

"That's *great* news!"

"Yeah..." she trailed off.

"You don't sound excited."

"I am. Really. I couldn't be more relieved." She hesitated. "I hate that he didn't trust me to begin with."

Mitchell sighed. "You could come back. We'll find you a new job."

She bit her lip. "If I'm starting over, I want to make sure I'm doing the right thing."

"What is it?" he asked.

"Nothing, I guess." She exhaled. "We can talk when I get home."

His tone brightened. "I'm looking forward to you coming back. I've got ideas! We could cut down a Christmas tree. Maybe dinner at the Space Needle for New Year's Eve. Just...take some time to enjoy each other, again."

She closed her eyes. The words sounded right. *So why did they feel so wrong?*

"Sure," she said. "We can do that."

"You sound tired—I'll let you go."

"Thanks."

"Goodnight."

"Night."

Molly slipped off her dress and pulled on an old T-shirt. After turning off the lights, she slid into bed, pressing the cool silver pendant against her fingertips.

Tomorrow, she'd have an answer. *Wouldn't she?*

Chapter Thirty-Six

Molly

She left the hotel early in the morning, overnight bag in hand. She reached the parking lot and looked back. It hit her. She might never see the Calypso again. Maybe for months—perhaps *forever.*

Returning home meant facing her future.

Would Mr. Maherson keep the project she'd worked so hard on? Would she still have a job? With Paul's lies exposed, she assumed her position was secure—but security wasn't the same thing as growth, and Molly had never built her career by standing still.

She pressed the button on the key fob, popped open the trunk of the car, and placed her garment bag, overnight bag, and the small box that had once held Jackson's Christmas gift inside. The necklace now hung around her neck.

She had everything she needed to go home—except for one last stop. She wanted to say goodbye to Ana.

The moment she stepped into Jackson's office, memories

flooded her. So much had changed since her first day in Serenity, Texas.

Ana beamed. "I'm so glad you came to say goodbye! I was afraid I'd miss you."

"Like I'd leave without saying goodbye."

"Well, you're heading back to your busy city life."

"Yeah," Molly said, quieter this time.

Ana's smile faded. "What's wrong?"

"I thought I'd be excited to go back."

Ana leaned on the desk. "You got everything you wanted. The Calypso gala was an immense success. Paul's lies were exposed. Your boss has to see what an asset you are." She paused, tilting her head. "Oh, honey, are those tears I see?"

"No," Molly said with a tight throat. "Something in my eye."

Ana pulled her into a fierce hug. "We're going to miss you, you know."

"I'm going to miss you too," Molly admitted.

"There's always a place for you here if you change your mind."

"But my life is in Seattle."

"Maybe. But there's an awful lot here, too."

They hugged one last time in silent understanding.

As Molly stepped back, Ana's eyes caught on her necklace. "It's beautiful."

"Jackson gave it to me for Christmas. He said I needed a memento."

"He's right. Don't forget us, Ms. Monroe."

"Is he around?"

Ana watched Molly's face. "Not today. I think he's taking a well-deserved break. He said he'll be in tomorrow."

Nodding, Molly touched the small Texas pendant at her neck and said, "I guess we got our goodbye."

Ana pulled her close for one last hug. "Honey, I don't think this is goodbye—just see you later."

She felt trapped in Texas. The drive to the airport felt twice as long, and unlike months ago—when everything had been arranged for her—she now had to return the rental car, catch the shuttle, and check her baggage before flying to Seattle.

As the shuttle wove through the highways and exits surrounding Bush Intercontinental Airport, she watched the scenery blur past. The sun shone on the palm trees and scrubby palmettos lining the roadside. The air smelled like a mix of humidity and smog. Nearby, the memory of stale coffee clung to the shuttle's fabric seats.

She glanced at the man sitting across from her. He was a slightly overweight man with tired eyes. He caught her gaze, forcing her to make small talk.

"Heading home?" she asked.

"Nope, off to New York on business," he said, puffing up. "I'm a pharmaceuticals rep. I have the highest sale in my company."

"Wow, you must have worked hard for that."

"Been at it for two decades." He smirked. "Two marriages didn't last near as long as this job."

"Well, I hope you have a pleasant trip." Molly turned her attention back to the window.

Her thoughts spun. Would she become that person in ten years? Flying to another city alone, leaving behind a husband, always choosing work over life? If she and Mitchell had married, would he have supported her decision to stay in Serenity for months?

Is this what she really wanted?

Being part of Ana and Jackson's world had made leaving harder than she ever expected. Seattle had everything she should need—book clubs, yoga classes, familiar coffee shops. But starting over there, without the connections she'd built in Serenity, felt...*hollow.*

"I'd rather keep the ones I have," she said to the window.

"Excuse me?" The man leaned toward her.

"Sorry. Just talking to myself."

He nodded and went back to ignoring her.

When the shuttle stopped, she hauled her luggage down the metal steps, digging in her purse for change to grab a luggage cart. She groaned as her phone rang.

With her hands full, she fumbled before answering on the fourth ring. "Hello?"

"Is this Molly Monroe?"

"It is," she hesitated. The number was a Texas area code, but she didn't recognize the voice.

"I'm sorry to bother you. Is this a good time?"

"I'm about to enter the airport to catch a flight."

"Ana said you might be hard to reach."

"You spoke to Ana?"

"Yes. I was hoping to talk to you about the Community Center."

Her heart skipped. "May I ask what this is regarding?"

"A job offer."

She blinked. "I've spent the past few months trying to keep the job I have. Thank you, but I'm not looking for a new one."

"Just one minute—that's all I need."

"Okay," Molly drawled, the same measured skepticism she'd seen from Jackson over the last few months slipping into her voice.

"I'm calling from Fusion Community Outreach in Coronado. We're a nonprofit focused on strengthening communities—nationally. We partner with municipalities, private developers, and media outlets to launch large-scale initiatives that bring visibility, funding, and long-term infrastructure support to underserved areas."

"Oh. If you have questions about the Community Center—"

"We're familiar with that work," the voice cut in smoothly. "But we're calling because of *you*. You have a rare ability to bridge corporate development and community impact. Our mission is to create national community awareness—coordinating partners, working with media and local businesses, and, most importantly, getting projects across the finish line. That's a skill set you don't find often."

"I'm flattered, really, but—"

"Can you just consider it? I can email you the details."

She hesitated before carefully spelling out her email address.

Once she hung up, she glanced between her luggage and the airport terminal. Within minutes, her phone pinged with the incoming email.

She checked her watch. There was still time. Quickly, she opened the message.

Chapter Thirty-Seven

Jackson

He'd just stepped out of the shower when he heard them—faint voices rising through the night air, like laughter threaded through a dream. Jackson rubbed a towel over his damp hair and moved toward the window, brows furrowing. Tiny lights blinked red and green across the front lawn beneath the soft glow of the street lamps. Rainbow strands wrapped around the railing, looping lazy patterns he'd strung with Ana last weekend—lopsided, a little chaotic, but cheerful as hell.

Then came the music.

Not music...singing.

Little voices, too many to count, stumbling joyfully through "The Little Drummer Boy." He padded barefoot through the house, the hardwood cool under his feet, pajamas clinging slightly from leftover steam. Somewhere out there, a reindeer statue bounced its head with mechanical determination. The whole thing screamed Hallmark fever dream. He was halfway convinced he was still asleep.

Skeptical and shirtless, Jackson flicked on the porch light.

The crowd that greeted him was not imaginary.

Children stood like a motley patchwork choir across the front lawn, hands cupping battery-powered candles, faces lit with the sort of joy that only sugar and mandatory group singing could muster. Parents lingered behind them, bundled in jackets, exchanging amused glances and warm cider in mismatched thermoses.

When his eyes found her, he couldn't breathe.

Molly.

She stood just behind the kids—knees locked, fingers twisted in front of her, like she hadn't quite decided if bringing an entourage of third graders to his house at night was wildly charming or mildly deranged.

His chest tightened. She was supposed to be in Seattle.

My God, she came back.

"Caroling? On a school night?" His voice was rough with disbelief, a low drawl he couldn't quite clean up.

She stepped forward, smile curling like dawn breaking. "They're singing by special request."

He stood—quiet and stunned—as she shrugged with all the guiltless mischief of a woman who'd just organized a suburban flash mob. "You need to stop making them do all your work," he said.

"I'd never," she said, holding his gaze like a dare. "They're just fantastic at it."

He didn't answer—not with words. He reached for her hand, his fingers folding over hers, grounding everything inside him that had been tumbling loose since the second she'd left his bed and disappeared back into the world.

"You're supposed to be in Seattle," he said again, more quietly this time.

"Well, you promised me a trip to the hill country." She said and shrugged. "I had to come back."

Still holding on, he tugged her closer. First a half step, then another, until her laughter was a breath away. "This must be a Christmas miracle."

"Might be." Her tone was light, but with an edge of reverence. There was something new in her voice.

His thumb grazed the chain at her neck, settling at the base of her throat where the necklace he gave her rested, silver winking against freckled skin still warm from the cold.

"I didn't get to give you a present," she said.

He pressed a kiss there, at that small vulnerable spot above the charm he'd chosen months ago, too hopeful, too certain. "So, what did you get me?"

She smiled—more heat than sugar—and leaned in, her voice a whisper just a breath. "Something I hope you'll like."

"From you?" He asked, like it'd be impossible to be disappointed. "I'll love anything."

Her soft laugh turned into a whisper. "I got you...me."

Before he could speak—before he could remember all the things he'd wanted to say if given another chance—she was on her toes, arms sliding around his neck. She kissed him like a promise, and he kissed her back like a prayer answered.

From the yard, tiny whoops and cheers rang out, and someone whistled. Jackson chuckled against her lips.

Behind them, parents herded kids toward minivans, car

seats beckoning and bedtime creeping. When the last voice fell silent and the battery candles dimmed into darkness, Molly pulled back.

His hands stayed at her waist, slipping just beneath the hem of her coat. God, she felt like home. His chest swelled so full it almost hurt.

"I'm staying," she said, with a shrug, like she wasn't shattering every expectation he'd dared to let himself believe in. "I have a new job."

His grin was instant and impossible to temper. "Has anyone ever told you that you give really excellent gifts?"

Molly laughed, a sound warmer than bourbon and brighter than the Christmas lights twinkling over their heads.

"Just you wait," she said, voice dancing somewhere between sin and sincerity. "I bought myself something, too."

His brow arched. "Yeah?"

She leaned up, lips brushing his ear. "Christmas-themed undies."

He groaned, then laughed, then groaned again. "You're gonna be the death of me."

He spun her toward the door, the porch creaking beneath their feet as he kissed her again, deeper now, now that they had time. All the time.

And in the quiet, Jackson knew. This wasn't just the dream he pored over while staring at makeshift blueprints, wondering what came next. This was his forever.

She had come back. Not because she needed him—but because she wanted to build something beside him.

And if she wanted chaos, career, holidays with construction

dust and caroling kids and mismatched socks in the dryer?

Hell, he'd give her the world.

She'd be the best partner a man could ask for. Smart. Fierce. Full of fire.

And she was his.

Game. Set. Christmas Match.

And come tomorrow, he'd find the tightest pair of mistletoe boxers he could get his hands on...for *balance*.

Epilogue

Molly & Jackson

"That didn't take long." Ana said. "Couldn't get you to see the handsome man in front of your face, and now wild dogs couldn't keep you apart."

"What do you mean? It's been at least three months!" Molly shook her head with a laugh. "And it feels like a lifetime!"

"Well, clearly this is for the best." Ana nodded her head and said. "I wouldn't want you, or Jackson, to die of old age before you could move in together."

"Thanks for helping unpack." Molly released a sigh and hugged her friend.

"What are friends for? I also sorted the rest of the boxes so you'll know which ones to unpack first and restocked the snacks in the fridge."

"You know, Jackson never appreciated you as much as I do."

Boxes lined the walls, making narrow walkways through the room. She'd left her mismatched furniture behind when Mitchell took his things. She couldn't see needing it—or wanting it—in her new life with Jackson.

"Right?" Ana grinned. "How are things with the new Coronado project?"

"It's actually perfect timing—and honestly, a perfect fit. The first phase is national rollout planning, so I'll be traveling constantly. It's part of the reason Jackson and I are moving in together now. It doesn't make sense to pay rent in Texas for the next three months when I won't even be around."

"How does Jackson feel about you being gone for the new project?"

"When has he ever not supported me? He says he's never been to Coronado and can't wait to visit."

"This job seems like a good fit for you. It's basically everything you're already good at—just on a bigger stage."

"Yeah. I don't think I ever would've gone looking for something like this, but it's funny how the best opportunities sometimes just find you."

"Speaking of surprises, Marco and I have a secret."

"Oh, tell me!"

"We're expecting a special gift next Christmas."

Molly clapped and squealed in delight. "No way! Ana, that's amazing!"

"Jackson walked through the door and interrupted them. "Really? Are you two back at it again?""

"Not this time," Molly said with a grin. "Ana's expecting!"

"What? And I'm the last to know?" Jackson feigned offense. He tapped Molly's nose lightly. "I'll remind you—I was here first."

Ana chuckled as she gathered her things. "Speaking of being here first, I need to go. Marco and I have a hot date night planned tonight."

"Thank you for your help today." Molly gave her one last hug. "Congratulations, again! We'll celebrate more soon!"

Ana waved as she left, and Molly shut the door before turning toward Jackson. "You haven't changed your mind? Are you still excited?"

"Absolutely. Now I can finally get some sleep without worrying about you sneaking off in the middle of the night."

Molly placed a hand on her hip and waggled her finger at him. "Come here, roomie, and give me a kiss."

His lips brushed against hers, his hands sliding down her back to cup her hips. "How was your day?"

Stepping back and looking up at him, she smiled. "Busy."

"Did he call again?"

"Not today."

"Do you think he'll try again?"

"Probably. Mr. Maherson didn't get where he is by giving up easily."

"Do you regret staying in Texas?"

"How can you ask that?" She bent to gather the papers into a neat pile, glancing over her shoulder at him. "What I'm doing now is just as important as my work with NorthStar Properties—only broader. National partnerships, media coordination, long-range development planning...just on a smaller budget."

"I know you have a plan for that, too."

"I've been mapping out grant pipelines, private-sector partnerships, and national funding channels—"

Jackson's lips covered hers mid-sentence. Pressing against

her, he teased the corner of her mouth with his tongue.

Molly laughed and tugged him toward the now familiar living room couch, making them both tumble onto it. "Should I talk grant proposals and fundraisers again?"

"Not unless we're staying in tonight."

Molly twisted around and sat up quickly. "The Spring Fling is at the community center!"

Jackson grinned. "The one and only."

"Beth convinced Ms. Sally's to cater. You know what that means—fried pickles."

"I almost regret asking Sally for help at the Calypso's gala. Is she even at the restaurant anymore?"

"She's still around, but not as much. You gave her a taste of the high life, and now she's busier than ever. Last I heard, she's talking about some sort of pecan pie and BBQ collaboration with Patty Cakes."

"Sounds like an unstoppable team...and an irresistible meal."

Molly stood and wandered upstairs to the bedroom. From the hall she called out, "The Calypso was good for a lot of people. I heard it's booking out months in advance."

"It was good for everyone...except Paul."

Molly poked her head around the landing, her shoulders bare. "He got what was coming to him. If I had my way, he'd be spending twice as much time in prison."

Jackson shook his head. "Can you believe he was embezzling from the company?"

Molly's muffled voice drifted from the bedroom. "After what he did to me? Yes. I'm just surprised Connor wasn't involved too."

A few minutes later, Molly strutted back into the living room wearing dark-wash skinny jeans and black cowboy boots.

Jackson let out a low whistle. "Maybe we don't need to go tonight after all."

Molly pulled him up from the couch and kissed him deeply. "This is what life's about. Now throw on your boots...I'm not missing another minute."

About Amber W. Lynne

An award-winning author from the misty, coffee-scented landscapes of the Pacific Northwest, Amber blends slow-burn tension, heart-tugging emotion, and just the right amount of sweet and heat into every story she writes. The relationships are relatable and her heroines are fierce, independent, and (sometimes) a little stubborn, but they always find the right man to love them.

Fueled by caffeine and an unshakable belief in love, Amber has been crafting stories since childhood, drawn to the way romance can heal, challenge, and transform. When she's not writing, she's playing with her five kids (I KNOW!), helping fellow writers embrace their literary dreams, or spending time with her hubby making a love story of her own.

<u>Ways to stay in touch:</u>

- Subscribe to her Newsletter

- Via email: info@AmberWLynne.com

- Follow on Instagram - AmberLynne.Author

- Follow on Facebook - Amber W. Lynne, Author

Also by Amber W. Lynne

Working For Love

Lanyards & Lariats
Toolbelts & Ties
Spreadsheets & Sprinkles
Gowns & Gavels
Bourbons & Bling
Holly & Heartbeats

Leave a review at your favorite retailer, and sign-up for Amber's newsletter, to get more love stories, sneak peeks, a chance at Beta or ARC reads, and exclusive giveaways.

To find more books by Amber W. Lynne, visit:
https://amberlynneauthor.com

Spreadsheets & Sprinkles

Working for Love, Book 3

Candy pounded the mound of dough onto the counter, her frustration evident in her grip. The lump of goo hadn't hurt her, but she needed to pound something else, or she'd start looking for someone. Unfortunately, she had no one to blame for her situation but herself.

She loved getting lost in the rhythmic work. Her hands skillfully kneaded a mound of dough with a rhythm born of years of practice. Flour floated in the air like a soft haze, dusting her arms and sweater as she kneaded with a force that wasn't typically required for baking. With each roll and push, her brow furrowed, and she resisted glancing at the bakery's financial ledger, which was open like a chasm on the counter beside her.

Patty's Cakes smelled of sugar, yeast, and a hint of vanilla—except the latter was in short supply. Her supplier had mixed up her last order. Again. Now, she was running out of time to adjust her baking schedule before the morning rush flooded in.

The tinkling bell over the door reset her worry loop. "Melanie! You made it." Candy looked at the clock hanging above the large picture window that faces Main Street. "You're a little late." She dipped her hand into the flour bowl and kept kneading the dough in front of her. "No worries. Can you start on the tarts?"

When Melanie didn't reply, Candy looked up. She stood in the doorway, shoulders rolled forward, fingers tightening around the strap of her apron.

"I'm sorry, Candy," she said, voice thick with guilt. "I can't work for free anymore."

Candy's stomach dropped. "Melanie, it's just a couple more days."

"You said that last week." Her face softened, but her voice didn't waver. "I wanted to tell you in person."

Panic clawed at her ribs. "I'll figure something out, just—"

"No, Candy." Melanie shook of her head, said, "I'm sorry," and then stepped back out the door and disappeared into the flow of early-morning shoppers walking down Main Street.

Candy gripped the counter, her pulse pounding louder than the hum of the fans over the ovens. Patty's Cakes was circling the drain, and she was running out of ways to stop it from taking the final plunge. She yanked her phone from the pocket of her flour-dusted apron and dialed the only number she had memorized.

"I'll be there in—"

"I need help," Candy said as soon as Bailey picked up, pressing her palm to her forehead, hoping to push back the pain gathering there. "Melanie just walked out. I'm drowning in numbers that don't add up. I'm not sure how much longer I can keep this afloat."

"You're ready?"

She hated doing this to her friend, but Candy had run out of options. Bailey had been trying to help her for months. The only thing stopping her from riding in with the cavalry and her family's ridiculous pile of money had been Candy's stubborn refusal of her help.

Now, Bailey's calm voice was a lifeline over the phone. "I was hoping you'd ask for help, and your timing is perfect. That guy I was telling you about, my old friend from high school and, now, accountant, is in town visiting his folks."

"An accountant? I was thinking more along the lines of you throwing on an apron and coming here to help man the shop."

"Candice Linn Brinley, you can't keep hiding from your problems."

"Bailey Ray Reynolds, don't you dare first, middle, and last name me."

"You know I'm right." Bailey sighed into the phone. "Things at the café have only been getting worse. I think he can help you."

"Maybe."

"You asked for help."

"A different type of help."

"You don't get to be picky about help, and you know the only help I can offer. These nails aren't made for piping bags."

Candy looked at the pile of dough that was forming a film and drying out. "I know. It's just really hard. My mom did this—"

"Alone, and you aren't alone. This has been going on for...I don't know...too long. When I heard he was coming, I was actually hoping you could meet."

"So, you were preparing to ambush me?"

"Overreacting much? Please." Bailey let out a long sigh. "I bet he could make sense of your books. Let me bring him by Patty's Cakes later. You'll love him. He likes spreadsheets, and he's got a knack for making things like this better."

"I need hands to help with things here, not math solutions."

"Fixing your finances *is* fixing the bakery." Bailey's voice softened. "Candy, you can't keep doing this on your own."

She didn't have time for emotions. Instead, she exhaled sharply and rubbed at her temple, smudging more flour across her face. "Fine."

"Fine?" Bailey asked, surprised.

"Fine," Candy repeated, defeated. "But if I don't like him, he's gone."

"You'll like him," Bailey said confidently. "I'll text when we're on our way."

Candy hung up, staring at her phone as if it had betrayed

her. She still needed help with the baking, and now she was letting a stranger dig through the wreckage of her books. Maybe this was just another crappy decision, but it couldn't make things worse, right?

Or maybe—perhaps—he could keep things from falling apart before they crushed her.

She turned back to her dough, rolling her sleeves up higher. It didn't matter who was coming. She needed to keep moving.

Mumbling to herself, she started kneading. "Patty's Cakes isn't going to save itself."

The bell above the door jingled again, and Candy looked up, expecting Bailey, but not the man standing beside her. He did *not* belong at Patty's Cakes. His broad shoulders and narrow waist looked like he hadn't eaten a pastry in his entire life.

Bailey flashed her a knowing grin. "Candy, meet Lincoln. Lincoln, this is Candy."

Candy's stomach clenched. He was tall, lean, and sharply dressed. A stark contrast to the flour-covered chaos she was experiencing. He looked neat. Precise. Organized. He radiated common sense and stability.

Lincoln extended his hand. "Nice to meet you. Bailey tells me you could use some help."

Candy eyed the hand warily before wiping hers on her apron and shaking it. "Some. I'm really fine. We're just a little short-staffed, short on vanilla, and short on..."

She shifted to turn back to her dough, misjudging the motion entirely, and before she could stop it—

Poof.

A violent cloud of flour exploded into the air, cascading down onto Lincoln's perfectly pressed suit.

Her mouth parted in horror.

Lincoln coughed once, then again, and then—without breaking expression—he calmly took off his glasses, wiped them with a precision she'd never learned to master, and placed them back onto his face.

Bailey pressed her lips together, failing miserably at hiding her glee.

Candy dropped the rolling pin and grabbed a towel, launching forward. "Oh my gosh! I am so sorry!"

He held up a hand as if to stop her from making the situation so much worse. "It's fine." His tone was measured. "Accidents happen."

Candy stopped dead, gripping the towel. "You sound like you get flour dumped on you all the time."

He said, "I don't."

Bailey clapped her hands together. "Well. This went well."

Candy still wanted to crawl into the nearest pastry display and never return. "Look, I know Bailey thinks you can help, but I—"

Lincoln's eyes flickered toward the half-open ledger. Even from a distance, even *covered in flour*, he seemed to see something in the mess of numbers that Candy had been dreading for months. His gaze was sharp, assessing. Calculating.

There was a long pause. Then, finally, he looked at her again. "You love this place."

Candy blinked. "Of course I do."

"Then let me help you keep it."

She wanted to say *no* out of instinct. Wanted to pretend she wasn't struggling as she watched her mother's business fall apart. Except...she was.

"Okay," she muttered.

Lincoln nodded. "I'll need full access to your records and receipts. And—"

Candy sighed. "Oh, this is going to be...so much fun."

Bailey bit back a laugh, and Lincoln—*stoic, flour-covered Lincoln*—stepped farther into Patty's Cakes, scanning the space like he already knew all the areas that weren't working.

Candy swore she saw the very *second* that he realized just how much trouble she was really in.

Yeah. This was going to be a disaster.

AVAILABLE AT MAJOR BOOK RETAILERS

RECIPE: Crispy Fried Pickles

Molly's Favorite Southern Snack!

Serves: 6–8
Prep Time: 15 min
Cook Time: 20-30 min

Jackson knew that if he was ever going to win Molly over, he'd need more than charm and a winning smile. Luckily, Ms. Sally took him under her wing and shared her secret to the perfect crunch. "It's not just the batter, sugar," she told him with a wink. "It's the patience—and the heart behind it."

INGREDIENTS:

- 1 (16-ounce) jar dill pickle chips or slices (drained and patted dry)

- 1 cup buttermilk

- 1 cup all-purpose flour

- 1 teaspoon paprika

- 1 teaspoon garlic powder

- ½ teaspoon cayenne pepper (optional, for a kick)

- ½ teaspoon salt

- ½ teaspoon black pepper

- Vegetable oil (for frying)

- Ranch, Spicy Aioli, Ketchup, or your favorite sauce for serving

INSTRUCTIONS:

1. <u>Prep the pickles:</u> Drain the pickles well and pat them dry with paper towels — this helps the coating stick and keeps them crispy.

2. <u>Soak in buttermilk:</u> Place the pickle slices in a bowl and cover with buttermilk. Let them sit for 10–15 minutes.

3. <u>Mix the coating:</u> In a shallow bowl, whisk together flour, paprika, garlic powder, cayenne (if using), salt,

and black pepper.

4. <u>Heat the oil</u>: Pour oil into a deep skillet or Dutch oven to a depth of about 1 inch. Heat to 350°F (175°C).

5. <u>Dredge and fry</u>: Remove pickles from the buttermilk, letting excess drip off. Dredge in the seasoned flour until well coated.

6. <u>Fry in batches</u>: Carefully place coated pickles in the hot oil and fry until golden brown — about 2–3 minutes per side. Don't overcrowd the pan.

7. <u>Drain and serve</u>: Transfer fried pickles to a paper towel–lined plate. Serve warm with ranch dressing or a spicy dipping sauce (like a mix of ranch and a dash of Ms. Sally's BBQ Sauce).

"If you can hear that crunch from across the kitchen, you did it right."

RECIPE: Ms. Sally's Secret BBQ Sauce

(Passed down, perfected, and never quite written down...until now)

Yields: About 2 1/2 Cups
Prep Time: 10 min
Cook Time: 30 min

Legend has it that Ms. Sally first made this sauce the summer her old high school sweetheart came back to town. She wanted something bold enough to impress him—and sweet enough to make him stay. It worked.

INGREDIENTS
- 2 cups ketchup

- ½ cup apple cider vinegar

- ¼ cup molasses

- ¼ cup brown sugar (packed)

- 2 tablespoons Worcestershire sauce

- 2 tablespoons honey

- 1 tablespoon yellow mustard

- 1 tablespoon smoked paprika

- 1 teaspoon garlic powder

- 1 teaspoon onion powder

- ½ teaspoon black pepper

- ½ teaspoon chili powder

- ¼ teaspoon cayenne pepper (optional, for heat)

- 1 tablespoon butter (for richness)

INSTRUCTIONS:

1. In a medium saucepan over medium heat, whisk together ketchup, vinegar, molasses, brown sugar, Worcestershire sauce, honey, and mustard.

2. Stir in the spices — paprika, garlic powder, onion powder, black pepper, chili powder, and cayenne (if using).

3. Bring to a gentle simmer. Reduce heat to low and let the sauce bubble softly for 20–25 minutes, stirring occasionally, until thickened and glossy.

4. Stir in butter just before removing from heat for that perfect, velvety finish.

5. Let cool slightly before using. Store in a sealed jar in the refrigerator for up to 2 weeks.

"Don't rush the simmer. Love takes time—and so does a good sauce."

www.ingramcontent.com/pod-product-compliance
Lightning Source LLC
Chambersburg PA
CBHW061231310726
48971CB00007B/2023